Winter Park

GRAHAM GUEST

Winter Park

GRAHAM GUEST

Published by Atmosphere Press
atmospherepress.com

Cover design by Nick Courtright
nickcourtright.com

10 9 8 7 6 5 4 3 2 1

Winter Park
2016, Graham Guest
www.graham-guest.com

dedicated to Winter Park Pub

Part 1

Eric Swanson

WINTER PARK

1

spring break **2000**

I am not an airplane. I cannot fly myself to Colorado. I have to get on a plane with other people, flown by other people, for other people. And for what other reason am I going to Winter Park than to see more other people? I suppose I could be going on a solo retreat to the mountains. I wish I were. But is that even true? I've been looking forward to going out to see these people for some time now. Apparently, they are important to me.

When I come back to Texas next week, though, it'll all be over, like nothing ever happened. Time will have just piffed by and no one will be the wiser for it; that is, unless I get really drunk and do something monumental and stupid. In that case the trip will be indelible, well, aside from the fact that I won't be able to remember the monumental and stupid thing I have done. Somebody might be able to tell me about it the next day though. If so, whatever they tell me I did will be something I will want to try hard to forget even though I can't remember it, so that right now I am about to go out to a place to do something monumental and stupid that I won't be able to remember but will nevertheless soon regret.

So, to relax, to settle my mind, just before boarding, I drink two double scotches and take a Xanax.

Planes are so uncomfortable, and this one, of course, is no different, and it's full of sick people; it's a flying tube of sickness, an airborne incubator of airborne influenza. If I had more than a week, if this were summer and I had a car, I would have driven, but it is only spring break, and that's all I've got to get up and back, a week, so I have to fly.

I always say, I'll never fly again, but I always fly again.

I do not know how to go about eradicating contradiction in my life. You'd think that I, being a philosopher, would be able to do it, or at least come a bit closer. But part of my charm is that I can admit my shortcomings. That's the best thing you can do: get your shortcomings out up front, set up a wall of disclaimers so that, in the end, when they come down on you, you can say, No see, like I said up front, I have shortcomings, and you were all on notice of them, and so you are prohibited from attacking me on those grounds.

"Gin and tonic please," I say to the male steward, who says nothing in return, except, "Five dollars." That's it: Five dollars - no, Certainly, My pleasure, or Sure - just, Five dollars. And I have no idea why I order a gin and tonic. In fact, I have never in my life ordered a gin and tonic.

The lady next to me looks at me askance.

Fuck you, I know, it's ten o'clock in the morning; I'm on vacation, I'm going skiing, I'm going to hang out in the mountains for a few days with a bunch of old drinking buddies and I'm having a fucking gin and tonic even though I've never had a gin and tonic maybe *because* I've never had a gin and tonic and just because of this shit I'm going to have fucking seven gin and tonics, yes, right now, just to piss you and that bitch next to you off, yes, because I am depraved and did you know also that I am a philosopher?

The plane bumps then plunges. I grab the lady's arm.

"Hey!" she says.

"Sorry, sorry," I say, sweat balls forming on my brow.

"Poon," the friendly tone indicates and Ted the pilot comes on. "Scone be bumpy. Buckalup."

"I'll have another G&T, please," I say, to a different steward, a woman.

"Sure Hon," she says and smiles, so much nicer. She pours all the stuff on the plastic and ice and hands it over to me. "That'll be five dollars."

"Comin' right up," I say. I lean over and add to her in a whisper that her compadre with the apron back there is not nearly as pleasant and as lovely as she and did she know I am going skiing and that I am a philosopher?

"That's wonderful," she says. She leans over and adds to me in a whisper something which I take to be about her letting Marcus know how I feel about him.

Concerned, confused, I grab her arm. "What? You wouldn't do that."

"Sir," she says. "You misunderstood. Now please let go of me."

The lady next to me pulls away to her right. I turn to her. "What?"

"Okay, that's it," the stewardess says, "we're not doing the gin and tonic right now. Here, give it back to me." She reaches for my G&T, I hold it away from her, over the lap of the lady next to me. "Come on, sir, give it..."

"Wait, why? What are you doing? I paid for this, it's mine. We have executed the transaction."

She leans all the way over me her right tit presses me in the left face she grabs hold of the drink it spills, "Shit!" I let go, she pulls away. "Marcus!" she calls down the corridor of the tube.

Marcus comes up and the nurse explains that I am intoxicated that I am being difficult but I step in and say that I am not but that in any case I am becoming aware of a potentially incendiary situation and that I promise to keep silent for the whole rest of the flight, and no more drinking.

They say okay. I take a little nap.

2

"Sir. Sir! Wake up!"

I open my eyes. There's a man in a blue suit standing over me, shaking my left arm, there is another man in a blue suit next to him, and then there is the stewardess, and Marcus.

"Here he comes," the first man says. "He's coming around. Yes. Mr. Swanson," he enunciates toward my face, "you are the last man on this plane. Time to get off."

"All right," I say clearing my throat and eyes and head. "Okay."

I grab my backpack and jacket out from underneath the seat in front of me, where they have been securely stowed, and am promptly escorted down the aisle.

How I had slept through the landing, and how those two bitches next to me had gotten by me without waking me up is nothing short of incredible. Wow, if there's a lesson here, it's got to be something like: Xanax plus three stiff drinks plus airplane ride equals deep shit.

The two blue-suited men lead me to a little white room with a one-way mirror deep in the terminal and tell me to sit in a blue plastic chair until they return. After a couple of minutes, my cell phone vibrates in my pocket.

"Hello."

"Socrates! What the fuck? Where are you?"

"Hey, you won't believe..."

It's Big Dave, but before I am able to let him know anything more about my predicament the second blue-suited man bolts through the door, snatches the phone out of my hand, snaps it shut, and takes it out of the room with him.

"I need to tell the people who are picking me up that I have been detained, *man*," I say loudly at the door. "Don't I get my one call? Come on."

Half an hour later, the first blue-suited man swings open the door. "All right guy. It's your lucky day. We're going to let you go. Come on. Get up. Right now. Get up."

I stand up.

"Karl!" he yells behind the mirrored glass. "Escort this bozo out of the building and get down to Terminal C, pronto!"

3

I get my cell phone back, call Big Dave, and head off through the airport to passenger pick-up...It's crowded, though to say that and mean it would be to go out on a limb because crowds can be relative to types of places and times and some places are always crowded whereas others are not and the airport is one of those places that is always crowded, but is that even true? Every night, especially in the wee hours, there's almost no one there.

Crowded is a crowded municipal train at five pm when people are packed in like sardines, sardines which also I suppose in a can are crowded, but dead, which prompts the question: is crowded a *live* condition or can a whole crowd be dead - and I mean literally *dead* not just passive - and still be a crowd? A dead crowd certainly does not *feel* crowded so to the extent that one needs to *feel* to be crowded one cannot be dead and be crowded and thus by extension one cannot have a dead crowd.

So, sardines are not crowded. But that's also not what people have been claiming about them all these years; people have been claiming that they're packed in; but there's a relationship between being packed in and being crowded: people, because they are alive, can be packed in *and* crowded; but sardines, because they are dead, can only be packed in. Though I bet there's someone out there willing to use crowded in the inanimate sense. She might for instance say, Those words look crowded on that page, please double-space. But are words really inanimate? Are words like dead sardines? Or can words, unlike sardines, successfully be crowded, in the animate sense?

When in use words certainly have more life than dead sardines, but what about when sardines lie dead and words lie dormant, which has more life? In dormancy words still differ from sardines because words when they are not in use are not dead forever; they simply lie fallow; they will be revivified in due course, maybe any second now. Sardines, on the other hand, when they are dead, they're dead and gone.

But is that even true? Because once, or rather *if*, I should say, a sardine is ingested and incorporated into someone's body and then that person uses words, isn't that sardine helping infuse and imbue that person and those words with life? It is certainly getting used to supply energy to that person and to the extent that that person needs energy to talk and use words well then the sardine is right back in there playing a part so even though it's dead it's *not* gone. Sardines then too, just like words, can lie fallow and available for future use.

Still, the energy from a sardine whenever it is used or ingested gets distributed and used up *on only one major occasion* whereas the energy of a word appears to be inexhaustible a word can be used over and over and over again and never run out of energy. That's a real difference between sardines and words. Another real difference is that people use words automatically and all the time whereas sardines, around here anyway, are not used automatically or all the time by any means; in fact, the word around here is, everyone hates sardines.

So let me back up. There are enough people in the airport today to make me uncomfortable, but then I have sociophobia so *any* number of people makes me uncomfortable. If I also had xenophobia claustrophobia agoraphobia and acrophobia I wouldn't even be at the airport right now, but since I only have sociophobia I just want people to get off of me; that's all I ask, Just get off of me.

Like parasites or leeches or ticks they get under your skin by talking; talking is their method of penetration; they stand in front of your face and talk until you listen then they look at you and you have to answer you have to say something and as soon as you do they're in you you're engaged and you can't shake free of them, ever; they've deposited a seed a germ a contaminant of themselves inside of you that you will carry around with you forever until you die and you will pass the disease of that person on to others you meet even to your own family until everyone has the disease of everyone else in them and we're all sick.

"Hop in, Bitch!" Big Dave calls through the passenger side window of the Outback.

I get in. Despite the cold, Big Dave is in shorts and a Hawaiian beach shirt.

"Dude, what happened?" he says, staring at my face, his mouth hanging open a bit.

"I was detained."

"Detained? For what?"

"Being drunk on the plane."

"Awesome," Dave chortles then adds, more thoughtfully, "It is so weird how, how unassuming you are, and yet you are always getting into so much trouble."

"Yeah, it is weird." I have to agree.

"But so no fine, no court date, jail time?"

"No, no, nothing, thank fucking god. But it could've been terrible...I mean...I think the punishment for something like that is fucking...but then they just up and let me go. I don't know why.... something about Terminal C. I don't know."

"Wow." Dave pulls back out into traffic, concentration on my recent escapades obviating his need to drive like an idiot for the moment. "Auspicious commencement to your vacation, to say the least though, fuck, huh?"

4

Winter Park is high. At over nine thousand feet, it is one high town. The only higher in the United States is Alma, Colorado, at over ten thousand feet, but since there are no businesses, and almost no living organisms in Alma, many, especially Winter Parkers, say the distinction of highest US "town" belongs to Winter Park.

Coming to this altitude means a couple of things. One is that, whatever time of year it is – it might be the middle of July – it can become winter at the drop of a hat. It could be one hundred degrees in Denver and twenty-seven and snowing in Winter Park. It's important to be prepared for that. The other thing is dehydration and high altitude cerebral edema, or swelling of the brain (people also get cerebral edema from physical injury to the head). You need to be very wary of these. They can have serious consequences ranging from impaired judgment to death. The universal antidote for both is water. Drinking water, at all times, especially during the first few days after arrival, and especially if you're drinking alcohol, is critical.

The approach to Winter Park from the south on Highway Forty, over Berthoud Pass, at eleven thousand three hundred feet, and down the north face of Colorado's front range, is treacherous. The road has numerous switchbacks and abysmal precipices over which to plunge to one's death, and it is, obviously, particularly deadly in the wintertime, which is to say, again, potentially anytime. But the mountains are breathtaking, aspirational. Parry and James Peaks, thirteen-four and thirteen-three respectively, to the east of town, top them all. Parry Peak, overlooking Winter Park from the east, wears a scar of three vertical glacial trenches on its face called "the bear claw".

The Winter Park area is also distinguished by its three tiers; most Colorado resort areas can boast only two: a ritzy resort tier, where all the money and tourists stay and play; and a nearby, lower-grade service town tier, where all the permanent residents - who very often work up at the resort – live. Take Vail and its service town, Avon, for example, or Snowmass and Carbondale. Winter Park, on the other hand, has a middle tier, the town of Winter Park itself.

As you come down off Berthoud Pass, you first encounter the Winter Park area ski and summer resorts, Winter Park Resort and Mary Jane Resort; a mile or two below those, you enter the town of Winter Park itself, population about six hundred and fifty; and a mile or two below that, you enter Fraser, population about a thousand. The resorts, obviously, occupy the top tier; the confusion is over which town is the service town. But by and by one comes to understand that Fraser, with its lo-rent condos, big box grocery, household, and hardware stores, hooker (i.e., tow-truck) service, and its own local bar, The Crooked Ferret, and breakfast joint, Sharky's, is the true service town of the resort areas and that the town of Winter Park operates in a middle, twilight zone between the two, somehow serving only itself. Winter Park is, in a word, a misfit.

Taking up two understated sides of only about a one-mile stretch of Colorado Highway Forty between the resorts and Fraser, Winter Park has several tolerable restaurants (though one has to understand that the taste of everything is neutralized at such altitudes), a post office, a public park, a campground, several bars (the most notable of which is the No Holds Bar and Grill – it is the heart of town), and three perpetually vacant motels: the Valley-Hi, the Sunsetter, and the Olympia (which is in that grand Swiss chalet style; the other two are just collections of wood and cinderblock boxes). I lived and worked in Winter Park for three years, so I was a true Winter Parker. My haunts were, at the far south end of town, the Valley-Hi, where I lived, all three years, and worked over the summers; at the far north end of town, the No Holds Bar and Grill, where I drank, a lot, all year round; and at the resort, Mary Jane Resort lift number eleven, where I worked over the winters, and did not ski, not nearly as much as I intended.

5

As Big Dave and I pass the resorts and head down into town, everything seems a little sad. Though everything doesn't just seem sad; it *is* sad because why should a sad feeling - or any feeling for that matter, however subtle or fleeting - be relegated to a mere seeming? Feelings, to the extent that we have to be conscious of them to have them, don't *seem*; they *are*. But that's just it: most of the time we are not consciously feeling anything at all; most of the time we just potter about on autopilot, but is that even true?

It probably is, actually. I mean, a person spends like what, one-third of his time asleep? So two-thirds of his time are spent awake, but awake doesn't necessarily mean conscious where by conscious I mean doing what I am doing right now: attending pretty fastidiously to a train of thought in the forefront of my mind; no, we all know the experience of going along walking maybe driving along and then out of the blue waking up from a protracted period in which absolutely nothing has been going on in consciousness nothing reflective anyway, at all.

Of course perceptually we have been performing automatic sensory monitoring in order to keep our bodies safe and on track, but this might be considered to be unconsciously controlled or automated behavior, and suddenly we're in the business of deciding, defining what unconsciousness is which is suspect because in my opinion it is a favorite human pastime to go about defining and delimiting things, phenomena that defy definition and limits in the strict sense, but now I am trying to say with authority that we cannot speak about such things with authority and that is certainly a problem.

In any case, I think some of the sadness I'm feeling is emanating from Big Dave. He hasn't changed since our undergrad days at Colorado University; he's still a giant galoot. I have changed; I've gone from insouciant mountain drunk to pensive and ponderous moral philosopher in one swift easy action. It was only six-seven months ago I was still living in Winter Park, skiing and boarding and drinking and working the lift at the mountain.

But so just where do I get off, then, calling Dave a galoot? Or calling him *still* anything? I have no right, no authority to call him anything at all, and yet I do this all the time, I characterize others absolutely as one thing or another in passing moments, in conversation or in private thought - whenever I am actually thinking consciously - as if I had access to such information. Maybe that's what's sad: this precipitous and specious characterization of others.

God, what is a person? Who is Dave? A collection of whatever he has meant *to me*? But what if what he has meant to me has been inconsistent? What if what he has meant to *himself* has been inconsistent? Well, we are in it then and I think we are.

6

"…But it's possible, Dave, that language itself, the Logos of the Cosmos, the supposed pathway to the truth of all inquiry, is actually the problem, that language, in all of its glory, is also an infinitely imperfect medium of uncertain origin and questionable destiny."

"Dude, it is not possible for me to follow you right now, and I refuse to try," Big Dave says. We crunch through newly fallen snow into a parking space just outside the front door of the No Holds Bar and Grill, my old stomping grounds.

"Would it surprise you if I told you I do not follow myself?"

"No. Now come on. Let's go."

"And that *that's* part of my theory? That no one understands himself, either, despite…"

"Dude." Big Dave shuts his door. "The tap awaits thee."

"All right. But you know I'm going to need to hydrate before too long here as well. I have not been at this altitude in a long time."

"Of course."

The moment I step across the familiar threshold and into the dark bar, I am swept off my feet, carried over to a nearby table, and deposited on my back, where above my eyes appears a Jägermeister bottle with a silver spout, over the tip of which someone's thumb is acting as temporary stopper.

The bottle descends and a voice says, "Open!"

So I open, the thumb comes off the spout, and the Jäger begins to flow in a cold black stream, directly into the back of my mouth. I swallow it as fast as I can, but it keeps coming and coming, and I wonder if they remember just how easily I get pounded, but it just keeps coming until finally I have to turn my head. The stream, however, continues to release onto my face and down my neck and onto my chest.

"All right, stop! Stop, goddamnit! That's enough!" I say. "Fucking let me up!"

Everyone cheers and hoists me back upright so I am sitting on the edge of the table, and Big Dave says, "All right then, what'll it be? And don't say Fat Tire! Don't carry it anymore."

7

I really know only a couple of the guys in the bar; the rest are mere acquaintances, or even total strangers, and I have to wonder, Who are all these people and why are they celebrating the return of someone they hardly or don't even know? And who did I think I was coming back here? Suddenly I feel awkward, but then Ted saunters up. I remember Ted.

"Peanut butter and jelly sandwich?" he says.

"Man, what is up, Slice-ington?" I give him a big hug.

We separate. He says it again. "Peanut butter and jelly sandwich?"

"Okay, what? What is that, man?"

"Remember?"

I do not.

"Dude, you were so pounded, and after trying to wrestle Nico, you came up to my place, when I used to live behind the bar here, and demanded a peanut butter and jelly sandwich, and then when you were eating it, all the jelly was falling out onto the floor, which I didn't care, but my housemate, Aaron – remember him? He got all pissed then you tried to wrestle him, and it seemed like you were joking around, but he was actually really mad, and he picked you up and threw you into the corner onto your fucking head! God! We thought you were dead for a minute!"

Ted's bleary eyes and gaping rictus attach to my face in good-natured anticipation, but all I can think to say is, "Wow, yeah. That's crazy."

"It was *awesome*," he says spilling his pint on my shoe.

"Dave. Dave!" I call down the bar. "Water!"

8

I wake up. It's dark, well, except for the silvery moonshine coming in through a large window. Actually I can see almost everything so to say it's dark, while of course correct, cannot be *exactly* right. I raise myself up onto my elbow. I'm at Big Dave's, on his couch. Ted is asleep in the beanbag chair with all of his clothes on, including his shoes, and there is no blanket on him; there is a blanket on me, which I do not remember getting, my shoes are on, and I'm wearing all of my clothes.

I sit up all the way. The couch is wet. Christ. I get up and look behind it. There are towels on the carpet. I press my right big toe down onto one of the towels. It squishes.

I go to the kitchen, fill up a glass with water, drink the whole thing down, do that three more times, go back to the couch and sit down at the dry end.

"Fuck." I exhale.

Ted does not move.

I lie back down. I lie sideways along the edge of the couch, careful to avoid the wet area, and stare out the window. Everything is silver and black outside.

9

fall 1983

I was ten years old way too old for mishaps with piss my room was like a black hole the carpet was brown and black shag the walls and curtains were thick dark green velvet there was no light in there especially at night this apparently was how my parents my mother saw fit to decorate my room in the middle of the night I woke up and had to pee I stood up and walked slowly blindly for the door I found it but could not locate the doorknob I felt up and down and sideways along the wooden door but could not find the knob so I walked back over to my bed sat down regrouped stood up and tried again for the door and again I found it but could not find the knob the situation was getting worse desperate I was starting to panic not only because I was unable to locate a doorknob I knew was there but also because by this time I really had to pee and the tip of my penis hurt and there was pee coming out of it I went back to my bed again and sat down almost crying maybe crying and made a critical decision I stood up and felt my way around the head of my bed to the little plastic pinball machine that sat close to floor in the corner you played it sitting on the floor I was peeing a little bit more all the time squeezing the tip of my penis *hard through my pajamas then I did it I had to I took out my penis and peed all over the pinball machine it was better to pee onto the machine than directly onto the floor because the urine was dispersed spread out evenly around the edges of the machine when the transgression was complete I shuddered with a relief so sublime so joyful so euphoric that any shame associated with the event was at least temporarily evaporated.*

10

spring break **2000**

I am awakened by the sound of someone rummaging around in the kitchen behind me. I stir.

"Well good morning little school girl," Big Dave says.

"Hey," I say. I raise myself up. Ted is gone.

"You remember peeing all over the place last night? You owe me a new rug and couch. Seriously."

"What? Shit. No. No, I don't remember anything after the bar. Fuck, I am so sorry."

"Yeah. You're way out of practice, especially at altitude, I guess. But man, you know, we probably shouldn't have dumped all that Jäger down your throat right away like that, either." May be. "So if you can just pony up a few bones for a Manley Steamer session on the rug and couch, like today, maybe we can call it even. How's that sound?"

"Yeah, sure. Whatever you want to do. I feel so ashamed."

"Oh, don't say that man. Shame is the coward's cocktail."

I have no idea what that means.

"But so Dave," I say coming into the kitchen area, "can you clear a few things up for me, then, about last night?"

"Sure. You left the bar by yourself, and when we got back up here, we opened the door and you were peeing on the couch. We tried to stop you, but it was too late. And that was pretty much it."

"Well, did I say anything or do anything else?"

"No. We tried to talk to you, but you were basically incoherent."

11

Dave makes up some scrambled eggs and toast for us. We eat. He says he has to get down to work; they're building a new stage at the bar. He showers and gets dressed. I make arrangements for the Manley Steamer guy to come by then stand over by the window and stare out into the snow.

"Come on down to the bar later," Dave says heading out the door.

"Yeah, sure. See you later," I say, I guess weakly because he says, "Hey. Is that a frowny face I see over there? No frowny face in Winter Park, big boy, okay? Take a shower; get cleaned up. You'll be raring to go again in no time."

I smile. "All right, dude."

I look around for my backpack. It's in Dave's car. I shower and get into the same clothes. I take my shirt off and borrow a clean one from Dave. The doorbell rings.

"Steamer," a man's voice says.

"Just a minute." I stand up. The doorknob turns, the door opens, and the guy just comes on in. He's a tallish, wiry, bearded fellow in a yellow jumpsuit.

"Hey," he says.

"Hey."

"You say you need the couch and the rug steamed?"

"Yeah, just the couch and the rug behind the couch, over there, right where you're standing basically, is all that needs cleaning."

He smiles. "Yeah, I understand."

"Yeah, so I have about $100 in cash in my wallet at the moment. Is that going to be enough, or...because if not, I'll need to get down to an ATM and get some more cash for you."

"Well, that's a start. I can give you a lift down when I'm done. There's an ATM at Suds."

"All right. Cool."

"Okay, well good enough. Lemme get my stuff and I'll be right back, get this piss cleaned up."

He comes back pulling a large silver suction hose that's hooked up to a machine in his van, and the whole contraption is making an incredible amount of noise. The guy works the carpet first then pulls the cushions off the couch and does them and finally does the back and bottom of the couch without the cushions. When he's finished, he puts the couch back together, returns the hose to the van, turns the machine off, and comes back upstairs.

"Man, don't I know you from somewhere?" I say.

"Yeah man. I was wondering when you were going to figure it out. I've grown a beard, and my hair, is probably why you didn't recognize me. But yeah man, it's Strock, Strock Futkins. You and I spent a little time hanging out up here, last summer I guess it was."

"Oh yeah. Fucking-A, man. How are you?"

"Good, dude, good. And yourself?"

"Well," I laugh and gesture to the couch and carpet,

"I've had better days. But I'm all right. I'm good."

"Well right on, man, cool." He bobs his head up and down a few times. "So. Down to Suds, then?"

12

"I know Suds," I say pulling the van door shut. "The beer, laundry, and video game place on the main highway."

"Exactly, dude. Exactly," the Steamer says. He puts the van in gear and we start off down the hill. "So, how's philosophy school treating you over in...where is it again?"

"In Texas. I'm in the Ph.D. program in philosophy at Rice University in Houston."

He puts his hand to his chin. "Hmm. Never heard of it. You sure it's a *real* place? I mean, what if reality is all an *illusion*," he says making little tickly motions with his fingers over top of the steering wheel.

I do not respond.

"Well come on, Socrates. I was serious. You're a bona fide philosopher now, so tell me: is reality all an illusion?"

I exhale. "Yes, yes it is. Our studies have shown."

"Fuck! I knew it, dude!" He's excited.

We pull into the parking lot. Behind the five-story skeleton of the ever-unfinished "luxury" hotel, storm clouds roll in from the northwest. It has already started to snow a little bit.

"They're never going to finish that thing, are they," I say, stepping out of the van.

"What thing? Oh, no dude. That thing will always just be a jungle-gym. They've never been able to make the luxury thing work here in town, only up at the resort."

We head down the stairs into Suds. I get two hundred dollars out of the ATM and hand it to him.

"Cool man. Thanks. Now at least let me buy you a beer, since you just overpaid me by a hundred dollars." He laughs. "Just kidding. But seriously. Lemme buy you a beer."

"Well, I was fixing to hook up with Dave…"

"Socrates. Come on now. You know Dave's at work. Let's grab a beer here then we'll head up to the bar for a visit. It's Winter Park, man. Come on."

Yeah, it's Winter Park, so I say, "All right," and we head over to the bar.

13

However, just as I reach down for the barstool the doors behind the bar swing open and a girl comes through them, puts her fists on the hips of her light brown corduroy pants and says, playfully, "Ah ha!" at which point I realize that the barstool I have already started to pull out and sit down on, because it's hooked onto the foot rail below, isn't going anywhere and that I am going to fall backwards, which I do, right through the table and chairs behind me and onto my back on the floor.

For a minute, there is nothing.

Then I smell shampoo, and a hand gently takes hold of my left bicep. Something, hair, clean hair, tickles my face.

"Dude, are you all right?" a girl asks.

I open my eyes. It's the girl from behind the bar. She's leaning over me, looking into my eyes.

"Of course," I breathe.

"Are you sure? Did you hit your head?"

"Yes, I did." I smile.

She smiles. "Do you want to get up?"

"In a minute."

She looks over her shoulder at the Steamer and says, "Whoa."

"Yeah," he says. "You all right there, brotha?"

She looks back down at me.

"Yeah. There is pain, but yeah, I'm fine," I say.

"Okay, here. Give me your hands," she says.

I do, and she gathers me up and helps me to my feet.

"I'm Eric, by the way."

"Nice to meet you, Eric." She laughs. "I'm Danielle. I gotta hand it to you, dude. You make one hell of a first impression."

"Likewise, likewise," I assure her.

Danielle is lithe and brown, her pants hanging boyishly on her hips below a bit of exposed abdomen as she stretches to tie her hair up behind her head in an imperfect twisty ball. Her breasts are small and perfect, tips pointing upward to the sky beneath a tiny purple t-shirt that reads, inanely, splendidly, in faded yellow letters across the front: Somebody In Colorado Loves Me.

"Well all right then," the Steamer announces, clapping his hands together on the counter in front of him. "Let's get back to the business at hand. First round's on me. So, we'll start with three Stellas and three shots of Patron."

Danielle, back behind the bar now, says, "Hey, that's really nice of you, but I'm going to pass."

The Steamer raises his eyebrows at Danielle then turns to me with them still raised. "No, no, that's okay. Times three, all the way around." He takes out his wallet.

Danielle shifts her weight. "No really, that's cool, Strock. I appreciate it, but you can count me out."

The Steamer stops. "You're serious. C'mon Danielle. Fucking Socrates over here's come up all the way from Texas for this."

She looks over at me then back at the Steamer. "No. Thank you, again, but I ain't doing it."

The Steamer pauses. Then, undaunted, continues his

campaign. "Okay, yes you are."

"No, I'm not."

"You are."

"Am not."

"Are."

"Not goddamnit! Now that's it!" Danielle explodes. "And don't you say another word, Futkins! Jesus, you gotta watch this guy," she says to me. She turns around to get the shots.

The Steamer leans over to me and whispers, "It's the other way around, brotha."

Then everybody is quiet for a little while.

14

The unfortunate exchange between the Steamer and Danielle ensures that the Steamer and I only have a couple of drinks down in Suds, and when we come up out of there, the snow is cascading down on Winter Park. We decide to walk over to the No Holds, but as we step up to the highway, about to cross, through a veil of falling snow he says to me, "Dude, actually, I'm sorry, man. I'm just going to have to run up the road to the Olympia here real quick. I totally forgot, I've got to meet some people, but I'll catch up with you down here in a bit, all right?"

"Yeah man." I don't care. "See you in a bit."

The Steamer runs off up the highway in the snow. I cross the highway and tromp down to the bar.

I walk in. It's just like old times.

"Hey!" I say. I belly-up to the bar, obviously feeling better.

"Dude, we only got like two hours of work in on the stage out back today before the snow got too heavy," Dave announces to me.

And I'm thinking, What stage? but say, "Yeah, it's fucking dumping," then remember about the stage.

"Yeah. So what'll it be? Smithwick's?"

"You're really trying to sell me on the Smithwick's, aren't you?"

"No, you can have whatever you want. I'm just saying, Smithwick's is good beer."

"I don't want Smithwick's. I'd like an ESB," I say, defiant.

"Sure. ESB's good beer too."

I sit with my pint of ESB and drink it as the bar swarms around me. I drink another. Then Nico comes in and pulls up a stool next to mine, puts her arms on the bar, orders a beer, and stares at the right side of my face until I acknowledge her.

"Oh! Hey Nico." We have a little hug. She's a tiny little thing. "You snuck up on me." She smiles. "Still over at Mountain Java?"

"Yes, of course. I heard you were in town."

"Hey Nico," Dave says. "You need a beverage? How 'bout some food? You guys want some food?"

Dave and I look at Nico. She's looking at me; she doesn't say anything. So, "Yeah," I say, "actually yeah. Chicken finger basket would be great, Dave."

"Okay, same for me," Nico says. "And an ESB, Dave, too, please."

Oh Lordy, here we go again.

Nico and I - just like Nico and every other guy who's ever lived in Winter Park - share a little history, and I do mean a *little* history because it only takes one time with Nico to know that there wouldn't – or at least really shouldn't - be another. "One Time" is, in fact, her nickname, born from a seemingly endless repetition of laments, such as, "Oh man, I did her one time, god help me," and, "One time I slept with her: never again," and, "It was only one time, dude, I swear," so it stuck.

Still, we try to be judicious in using the nickname

because we don't want to hurt her feelings, because it's true, she's just this really cute, sweet little mousey chick from Nebraska who works at the local coffee shop. But man, if you slept with her, well that'd be it; you'd never hear the end of it, not until the next guy blundered along to take your place. She is *so* needy, a real glommer-on-er.

So a real, tangible fear I have as she sits next to me, boring a hole into my face, is that, since our "one time" together last summer - and despite the fact that I apologized to her and she had said it was all good - the next guy has not yet blundered along to take my place.

"So Eric," she says. "I was wondering how you find Texas?"

"Ah. Well you see, Nico," I shoot the obvious gap. "Texas is rather large, so all you have to do is head straight south on I-25 out of Denver then just take a left at Albuquerque. You'll run smack dab into the side of it in no time."

Nico slaps my arm. "You suck, Eric."

Our chicken fingers come.

"Thanks, Dave," we say simultaneously.

Nico looks at me.

Christ.

"Of course, enjoy. Another round?"

We nod, Oh yes.

We eat for a minute. The beers come.

"Actually," I say, trying to be serious, "I find that Texas sucks."

She bursts out laughing. She starts coughing. She's having a coughing and laughing fit. She reaches out and touches her left hand to my right thigh as if to say, Help, I'm choking here.

"Jesus," I say. She rocks back on her stool; she raises her

right hand to her chest. I take her glass and hold it out to her. "Here, have some beer."

She ignores it and grabs the edge of the bar with both hands instead. "Hoo!" she says, her eyes watering. She indicates her throat and smiles. "Okay, okay. There was a piece of..."

I am still holding out her beer for her. She takes it.

"Nico, okay?" Dave inquires.

Nico takes a sip of beer and places it back on the bar. "Okay, yes. Okay. I am okay now. Eric. I don't know why that was so funny."

"Why what was so funny?"

"About Texas, silly!"

"Oh right. Well, maybe because it was true."

"You were being sincere?"

"Yeah. And it felt good."

"So why does Texas suck, then, Eric?"

"Well, don't get me wrong. It's not my philosophy program. Or, my philosophy program sucks, but in a completely different way because it's so hard to do well, and it takes so much work, and you're never certain whether or not you really understand what it is you're thinking and saying. But it's the whole state of Texas I was talking about. It's like the whole state is just one giant narcissist. Shit, it might even be a psychopath."

Dave has paused to listen. "Dude," he says, "how can a whole state be a psychopath?"

"I don't know, but just because we've never thought of it like that before doesn't mean it can't be true."

"Explain, but quickly."

"Well, I assume that there is a certain psychological profile, certain conditions that a person has to meet to be defined by mental health professionals as a psychopath, right. So, if you can get enough mental health professionals to agree that Texas fits the psychological profile of a narcissist, or a psychopath, or even a serial killer, then maybe that's it, that's all you need."

Dave stands there for a second. "All right," he says and takes off down the bar.

I look over at Nico: just staring at me. "So Eric," she says. "I have to ask. Have you been seeing anybody these days?"

The next thing I know, I'm standing out back at the bar in the falling snow, fucking kissing Nico.

15

winter 1999

I woke up in the middle of the night, still drunk, and naked, in Nico's bed, with Nico, and she was naked too. A bolt of hot panic fired through my body: if we'd had sex, I was none the wiser.

I took a deep breath. Yeast.

There was a glass of water. I took it and drank the whole thing down. Nico stirred. I hunkered back down into the sheets and closed my eyes.

Nico got up and went to the bathroom. Her piss was light and sprinkly, like a bird's. She came back and got into bed. I passed out.

A bolt of panic woke me up in the morning. I stirred. Nico made a little "hmm" sound and tried to roll over onto me.

"No, no. Nico," I said, scrambling out from underneath her and onto the floor. "I've got to work today. I gotta go."

16

It was snowing as I made my way down to the shuttle stop, and it was dark and gray and cold.

I stepped up into the bus.

"Hey Eric," the driver said.

"Hey Martin," I said.

"Getting some nice snow this morning, eh?"

"Oh, yeah, definitely." I sat down in one of the blue seats.

Up at the mountain, I stepped off the shuttle. The chairlift hummed with power through the falling snow. It was not crowded. I walked up to the lift attendant station and went inside.

When I stepped out, the lift-operator, a new guy, Matt something-or-other, said, "What's up, man? You on now?"

"Yep."

"Sweet." He handed me the broom, jogged over to the lift shack, grabbed his board, strapped it on, hopped onto the lift, turned around in the chair and said, "My turn," as he floated away up the mountain.

I stood out in the cold and snow for four hours sweeping off seats and occasionally helping people onto the lift. Sometime after 4pm, when the summit and I were sure everyone was off the lift, we shut it down, and I walked back to the shuttle stop.

"How was it out there?" Martin said.

"Great," I said, sarcastically, though he wouldn't have known it.

"Bluebird day tomorrow."

I stepped off at the stop in front of the No Holds, bid farewell to Martin, and went in for a beer.

I sat down next to Ted and asked Dave for a Red Hook ESB.

"Powder day tomorrow, eh?" Dave said as he tapped my ESB.

"Yeah, for those of us who can get up out of bed during the daylight hours," I said.

"I know," Dave said. "I hardly get up anymore...I mean, on the mountain."

Ted laughed. "Yeah, that too."

The bar door opened behind me and Ted.

"Hey Nico," Dave said.

17

spring break **2000**

I think better of getting any more involved with Nico and tell her I have to go. I say goodnight and walk out of the bar. It's stopped snowing. The Steamer, back in his Manley van, drives up. He rolls down his window. "Socrates, dude, hop in, man."

I do.

"Sorry about bagging out on you earlier, bro."

I shrug.

"Where you headed?"

"Well, I was fixing to head on back to Dave's, I guess, get some rest, maybe hit the slopes in the morning."

"You don't sound too sure about that."

"No. I'm not. Dave has to close at the bar tonight so I'd basically just be sitting up there by myself."

"Well, you want to head over to a couple of friends of mine's place in Fraser for a little while instead, have a beer?"

"Yeah man, I guess so. Sure. Do I know these people?"

The Steamer puts the van into gear and heads out of the lot. He takes a left at the highway and heads northwest toward Fraser.

"I don't know. I don't know if you know them. They're a couple I met up here a few years back. They've lived up here a long time."

"What do you mean, 'a couple'?"

"You know, a couple-couple."

"If you say the word twice, does that mean I am supposed to think of what you think I should think is the most common denotation of the word pronounced only once?"

"What? Man, I don't know how you can get drunk and talk like that."

"Well, you know how it is: Yo soy el rey." I laugh. "Sorry, man. I'm sure it's annoying."

"No, it's cool. I dig it. Their names are Bobby and Molly Nababadama."

"Really? Nababadama?"

"Yeah. Bobby and Molly Nababadama."

"Where are they from?"

"I don't know man. Maybe Germany?"

I don't think so.

We drive along for a few moments in silence.

"I actually met them at the No Holds," the Steamer says.

"Mm, I guess that means they're certified then."

"Certified Grade-A Winter Park beef."

"Nababadama Certified Grade-A Winter Park Beef Company." We laugh. We take a right off the highway, climb the hill into the cold darkness, and drive on for another few minutes until the Steamer recognizes a mailbox and takes another right onto a dirt road. We drive up that road for about two minutes and stop in front of a condo. Like so many condos in the region, the living area is up on the second and third floors, on top of the garage, accessible only by the steps on the outside of the house. A light is on in the big window.

"They appear to be in," says the Steamer.

'They' - two people, by testimony from the Steamer; 'appear' - not as in 'show up' so much as in 'look from all the evidence (i.e., the light in the window) discernible from this vantage point'; 'to be' – as in currently situated; and 'in' – as in contained within a sub-structure within the world, within the universe, etc. Thought about differently, though - maybe more literally, less colloquially - we ascend the icy steps - the words could mean, when strung together like that, something related, but also quite different. They could mean: 'The couple of people in question appear, i.e. show up, in the world *in order to* exist within structures and substructures of the world at large'. I am Martin Heidegger. The Steamer knocks on the door. I am a phenomenal logist. The door opens.

"Hey Strock," a giant hippie says. "How are you, man?"

"Hey Bobby. Good. How are you?"

"Good. Hey dude, what's up?" the giant hippie says to me as we step through the threshold of his domain and into the smell of drugs and cheap tacos. "My name's Bobby, and this is my wife, Molly."

"Hey, I'm Eric. How's it going?"

"You guys want a beer?" Molly asks from the kitchen area, which is situated behind the couch in the living area.

"But of corn," I say, a little joke. No one laughs. I take the Fat Tire.

"You guys want to drop tonight too?" Bobby asks the Steamer. The Steamer looks at me. I shrug my shoulders: Drop? Drop what? The bomb? My pants? Everything? What?

"I ask only because I have some of the most beautiful and potent liquid acid right now. I mean, you just would not believe the clarity of the shit. It's like twenty-four carat acid. No come-down; just pure fun."

I've taken acid before, a couple of times, but never liquid acid, and never twenty-four carat liquid acid, and I have just enough beers in me to make saying yes a real possibility; but I'll play it by ear; then again, there's no getting around playing it by ear no matter what I decide, is there?

We sit down on the couch and the giant hippie produces a huge bong from around the side of the couch and bubbles at it. He hands it my direction. I bubble at it a second and pass it on to the Steamer. Bong hits are not really my thing, but I do want to pursue the liquid acid idea.

"Hey," I say to the giant hippie, "I might be interested in your liquid proposition."

"Oh really? Sure, of course. Molly, you want to grab the dropper   from   the   el   cabineta   for   us?
"La cabineta," Molly says, smiling. "Here you go, honey." She hands Bobby a Visine bottle.

Bobby takes it, inspects it, then, holding the bottle up between his thumb and forefinger, looks at me and says, "Liquid-Crystal-Tele-Vision." My heart begins to race. "We don't put this stuff in or on anything but ourselves when we ingest it. You don't want to contaminate the magic. Just place a drop or two on the skin between the back of your thumb and your first knuckle and lick. You'll taste the vision, Eric. Here, hold out your hand."

The giant hippie drips out two viscous globes of silvery liquid LSD onto a patch of skin on my right hand.

"Well, here goes the neighborhood," I say then lick.

18

It becomes dawn immediately and with it across the big window fourteen eagles in formation fly against a silver sky, I stand paling in the light, watching disappearing, everyone else is already gone.

"I did the same thing," the Giant says startling me in the dark, I'm not sure, I say anything, "That window was my television," his presence makes me nervous, I think, he's standing near me, looking out the window with me, "All right, man, I'll leave you to it," he disappears into the dark grottoes of his habitation, places I do not want to go.

Some sections of me go to the fridge, open it, the light that comes from it is yellow filthy, it smells unholy but I reach in through it all, a locker of shit, and take out another beer, I look for hard liquor on the counter too but see only colored objects jumbled together ultimately however I am able to decode a bottle of Jim Beam, Jim, my old friend, I reach out and sever you from your place in the background I drink from your neck I carry you with me wherever I go.

It is a constant dawn, a perpetual dawn each time I blink when my eyelids raise comes slowly up the dawn again silver and pale and cold and unforgiving like the lights on stage are in an inexorable state of coming up from nothing but getting almost nowhere in their ascent, always only in a slow wow dissipating evaporating back to curtains drawn then lifting again like peek-a-boo in slow motion gone on forever.

Fuck, I'm blinking my way through, bathing in a sort of monotonous awe for ages it seems I am part and parcel of the objects in which I operate encased enmeshed infused imbued with whatever is made possible by them but which at the time for me is almost nothing, for me everything is nothing but something like an ongoing disappearing act.

I stand in the big window disintegrating in the razor thin light of my constant dawn, maybe there's something like relief in this, in this being relieved of all things determinate, but mostly there is horror, I'm still alive, buried alive in life in this house out here already dead, I inhale a current of chalky air into my lungs from the universe of chalky air around me it is a wonder I have not yet suffocated but we are all suffocating we all die of suffocation complications from suffocation eventually we all get seventy years it takes on average seventy years to suffocate to death from all the chalk in the air it takes about that long to fill the lungs and blood with dust.

I find myself out of doors behind the Giant's house maybe back behind somewhere crackling around in the cold moonlight there are darker shapes than the darkness itself moving through the darkness and then again becoming one with it indistinguishable I crackle over snowy ground and stand by trees as long as I don't call attention to myself I discover that my cell phone is vibrating in my pocket, and with it shakes loose the gestalt in which I am rapt.

A flush of ordinary emotion, anxiety, pulses through me, and I see things the way I did yesterday. I see that the way I am seeing things now is not the experience of the discovery of the essence of things; it's just the experience of another appliqué. There is no essence; essence is a myth; there is only existence, the cell phone is so small it's like a hard silver raisin in my hand in my palm and it grumbles at me from there it says, "Nico calling."

I look at it, blink at it, until it stops. Then suddenly defiant I transfer the unit from my left hand to my right, wind up and throw, it disappears from my hand, as far as I can up the mountain I long after its invisible flight into the snow and rocks and trees until I hear it snap on a distant stone, god, I laugh, it's dawn again, I turn around.

A yellow light more stain than light has come on inside the house, revulsion swells, hot and fat, it dissipates I'm dissipating chemical reactions but what is the connection between chemicals and experience they're inconsistent metaphors that have the same object I do not think we can know there are limitations here, where, when should I stop thinking is a normative question, it's up to me, and to all of those things that influence me without my knowing a figure comes out onto the landing of the wooden stairs it has to be the Steamer based upon the shape of things another human being why now just when I am feeling free there's always someone else fuck his hand goes up like a sound I think I hear it through the granulated air between us I re-place my feet and shoes in the snow and raise my hand up too it's silent, yes, my hand is silent but I want to yell out across the open mountain slope something something something like yo fuck off I'm fine welcome I look forward and do not to needing you later I am here.

The Steamer goes back inside the house I hear the tiny snap of the door from up upon my slope I am alone again except for the idea of him it keeps impressing itself upon me if I climb up the mountain further I will over time forget it unless I get hung up I have to shake my ideas I place my shoes and feet up on the mountain and go, it is dark but soon it will be dawn again.

I am surprised when I discover that Jim is still in my hand, he is in my hand, I sit down on a large smooth exposed stone and drink, it's sick and hot and poisonous and good, all the buckles and wrinkles are smoothed over by Jim, Jim, I feel something like love and perfection sitting with you here watching the sun come up over and over and over again because it is brighter when I have my eyes closed than when I have them open. I close my eyes, bright peach; I open them, still dark, but dawn has arrived, yes, I can tell by the birds, dawn has arrived.

19

"Dude, put your coat on. It's cold," the Steamer says handing me a shadow.

"And, and there was a formation of eagles, fourteen eagles. I counted them," I tell him, pointing over the top of the houses.

"That's awesome." He zips up my coat.

"They're not there anymore, man."

"Okay. You want to come back inside now?"

"Ah. I do not. But something tells me I should. All right. Play time's over, I guess."

"Man, it's just cold and you might need some water, maybe something to eat."

"Eat? Nah. Dude, I am now on board the all-day drunk train."

The Steamer holds onto my arm we start down the mountain I blink the big window curtains are open it's dark "Dude, what time is it?" I ask there is no answer I'm on the couch I close my eyes a band of horses charges through my face, I open my eyes, "Eric, man, be quiet. There are people trying to sleep," the Steamer whispers.

"What?" I ask propping myself up on my elbow. "Where are you?"

"You keep talking, but everyone else is asleep. Now go to sleep."

WINTER PARK

I'm standing in the kitchen drinking we're in the van the sun is coming up God what is happening the Steamer is upset he's driving straight ahead he's tired we pass Dave's car in the parking lot of the No Holds I tell the Steamer to stop he does I grab my backpack out of Dave's car "Yeah" I say "yeah" holding it up in the air for him to see.

The Steamer drives the van around and around on a sort of a circling loop like a circular freeway entrance that just keeps circling upward and upward like a corkscrew but never merges onto the freeway I am wrapped in a blanket like a king looking sideways out the windshield of my face when we stop going round in a circle we're parked, outside the Valley-Hi "Come on" he says "Come on" I say I slide out of the van and into to the room the Steamer's gone it's dark except for a silver sliver of static shaking in the shape of a wire in the far corner next to the window.

20

early summer 1999

I took Jim by the neck and shuffled in my underwear over to the window. I opened the shade and ripped into a huge slug. As the bottle was tilted up and I was dumping its contents into my mouth, a family of three - a father, a mother, and a daughter of some small number of years - walked by outside. They looked in at me and hurried on.

I set Jim on the bedside table and sat down on the inside edge of the bed. I was the last frontiersman, and it was stark and bleak and flatter than shit.

"I am going to die out here like this," I said and the telephone rang.

"Fuck." I stared at the phone.

It rang again at full volume.

"Fuck!" I picked up the receiver, if only to keep it from ringing again. I held it in the air in front of me. I heard a tiny voice.

It said, "Hello...hello." It was a girl. I brought the receiver closer to my face.

"Hello?" I asked toward the plastic hole.

"You're a bastard!" she yelled - it was Nico – and hung up.

I put down the receiver in its cradle, grabbed Jim, spun off his cap, stabbed his glass neck back into my mouth, and drank.

"Ah," I said to the phone, "that's better," and then it rang again.

"Fuck!" I picked it up. "What!"

"Socrates. Swanson," a guy said.

"What. Who is this?"

"Strock, dude."

I blinked. A blade of light was slicing through the curtain into my eyes.

"Hold on a second, man. Hold on."

I set the receiver down on the bed, went over, and pulled the curtain tight.

"All right," I said, sitting back down.

"So dude, you partying tonight?"

"I'm partying right now, bitch."

"Well don't party too hard. Wait till I get off work, okay? I'll come over."

"Uhh, I'll see what I can do," I said, looking at Jim.

21

late summer 1999

It started to rain, a beautiful, cool mountain rain. I pulled a chair up to the foot of the bed, in front of the TV, and switched it on. I clicked around the channels until I landed on what appeared to be the Olympics. It was the Olympics. I had no idea. I leaned my chair back against the bed, balancing on two legs, and held Jim by the neck as various countrymen ran the hundred meters, and threw the javelin, and the rain came down on the roof, a deluge of a billion pellets from the sky. I was the last frontiersman all right.

I woke up to the sound of someone knocking at the door. I was in bed. The TV was still on. Jim was next to my head on the bedside table, almost exhausted.

"Yeah. Coming," I said. I got up and opened the door. It was Old George.

Old George came in and sat at the table near the window. I got back in bed but sat up with my head against the wall. I turned the volume down on the TV.

"Not much to do around here, with the rain," he said looking out the window. "In fact, I was thinking about heading up mountain tomorrow morning to do a little camping." He turned towards me. "You think you can look

after things around here for me for the next couple of days, until Sunday afternoon? You going to be around? You're heading outta here for good pretty soon, aren't you? Off to Texas? Rice University?

I nod. "Yeah, I am, but my flight's not until late Sunday night, so I can cover you."

"Right. Okay, well that's perfect then. Oh, and listen, if you would, tomorrow morning..." He raised an eyebrow. "I'd like you to clear the front walkway. There's a lot of mud on it from all the rain. Okay? How you doing, Eric?"

"Pretty good. Watching the Olympics."

"The Olympics," he echoed, looking at the TV. He looked at me. "You seem pretty drunk, Eric."

"George, that is a distinct possibility, but I don't have to work today. Do I?"

"No, not today. But what if there were an emergency?"

"What do you mean? What kind of emergency? Like save the kids from drowning, avalanche?"

Old George laughed. "That's an old trick, asking for examples, and I'm not going for it."

"Or a fire? What if there was a fire?"

Old George laughed again. "Yeah. Well..." He looked out the window into the rain. "I just hate to see a good young mind go to waste out here. It's a story, a short story, I am all-too-familiar with." He turned back to me. "Eric, like you, I came out here after I graduated from Colorado University, worked the lift at the resort during the winter, and worked here, as groundskeeper, during the summer. But mainly, I was just a partying ski-bum. What was in the back of my mind to do the whole time, though, was play music, get out and peddle my tunes to people. Granted, I played around here for folks a little bit, but mostly it's just something that remained a dream in the closet. And that's where it remains today."

George sat back and looked out the window again, his yellow-gray hair and beard paling in the flat light. "See? Short story."

"I don't know, George. I feel like you can still get out there and peddle your tunes to people. I don't think it's ever too late for that. Shit, you can always get a night up at the No Holds. They'll let you play. And I don't know if you know, but it's really cheap and easy to make an album of your own music nowadays."

"Yeah, well, look," he said getting up. "Just don't waste your life and your dreams sitting around getting drunk and hanging around with a bunch of idiots, like Futkins. It offends the sensibilities. And don't forget to clear the mud from the walkways, in the morning."

"I'll do it. I'll take care of it, for sure, in the morning."

He forced a little smile. "All right, Eric. See you Sunday." He walked toward the door.

"Oh, George. Before you go. I just wanted to make sure, if I want to camp in the campground while you're gone, you said use number six, behind the manager's office, right?"

Old George paused. "That's the one I use. No one ever wants that one."

Old George opened the door. Strock was standing there with a case of Bud Light in one hand and a bottle of Jim in the other. Old George shook his head and pushed past him.

Strock came in and shut the door. "Man," he said, "I fucking hate that guy."

22

spring break 2000

I wake up. It's afternoon. Everything's a blur, but I don't feel too bad, not as bad as I should, and I know where I am: I'm in my old room, at the Valley-Hi. I shower and get into some fresh clothes. I open the door to go, but the Steamer's coming down the hallway at me. He's brought Jim with him and a twelve-pack of Heineken.

"Dude, get back in there," he says. He pushes me into the room with the alcohol and drops it onto the table. "Now, I understand, you might be a little tired from your escapades last night, but this awesome band, Weirdo, is playing down at the No Holds in a few hours. It is a special occasion for which we must make proper preparation. Therefore, I have procured for us a special treat, a little surprise."

My heart sinks and soars. I know what it is. He reaches into his pocket, pulls out a fat little bag of coke, and dangles it in the air.

"Dude," I say. I close the door to the hall but stay close to it, by the bathroom.

He bounces his eyebrows sexily.

"Man, I was just heading out. I want to say hi to Old George, and I got to get something to eat."

He continues with the eyebrows.

"I really should, dude. He's an old friend, and I owe him a favor, from last summer."

He stops with the eyebrows. "All right, whatever you say, boss." He throws the coke onto the table. "But he's not here."

"What? Really?"

"Nope. There's a note on the office says he's gone out and won't be back until later tonight."

"Oh. Well. Was he here last night? Didn't somebody check me in?"

"You mean this morning, and no, no one checked you in...Listen to yourself. This is the Valley-Hi, in Winter Park. Dude. Socrates. I know you had a long night last night, but come on, help me out here."

"What?"

"Dude, you still have the keys. They were in your backpack? Remember? You said it was cool."

"Oh. Shit." I reach into my pocket and take my keys into my hand. I hold onto them. I let go. "Well...There's nothing I can do about it now, not right now anyway. The old man will have to wait."

"Exactly, dude," the Steamer says. He pulls a chair back from the table for me. "Fuck Old George."

23

The Steamer and I walk up to the No Holds. The band is playing. I open the door.

"Dude," the Steamer says. "I don't have my wallet." He's holding his ass.

I close the door. "What?"

"I left my wallet, and my credit card, in the room, next to the TV."

"Well don't worry about it now, man. I'll spot you. Come on."

"No, no, that's cool. I gotta have my wallet. You go ahead. I'll run back."

"You sure? You're gonna miss the whole first set."

"Yeah, I gotta have my wallet."

"All right." I take my keys out of my pocket. "It's this one."

"Cool." He puts them in his pocket and pulls out the bag of coke, or whatever it is – the shit is strong, way stronger than usual. "Here," he says, hands it to me, and runs off, back up the hill.

I open the door.

Weirdo are four bushy-headed, bushy-faced dudes who are not young anymore but still sound good. They've got a sort-of southern sound with elements of jam, like they were brought up on seventies rock - though are not old enough to have been teenagers in the seventies - and there's something both familiar and strange about the lyrics, what I can understand of them. They are a new classic rock band; they are a southern jam band, and I like them more and more as they go on.

Ted, sort of as usual, no matter who is playing, is right up front, swinging around, slinging beer out of his pint glass all over the floor. I stand down at the end of the bar for the whole set and watch and listen. During the break, I step out back for some air.

"Aren't you cold?" a girl's voice asks behind me as I stand at the fence, gazing into the snowy pines.

I turn around. "Danielle! Hey!"

"So, how's your head?"

"How's my...How's *my* head? How's *your* head?" I try to correct her but do not know what she is talking about.

"No dude, from your tumble yesterday, down at Suds."

"Oh." I reach for the back of my head and remember. "*That*. Yeah, well, I guess I'm either fine now, or I have brain damage...or both."

She laughs. The music starts up again inside.

"These guys rip," she says.

"Yeah, totally."

A shadow flashes by and there's a quick, violent motion in front of us, the result of which is a whole pint of beer splashing into our faces and all over our clothes.

"You bastard! Fuck you too, Danielle!" Nico says and stomps off, out the back gate, into the snow.

24

Danielle decides to call it a night and head back to her place to get cleaned up. I try to explain and to get her to stay for a while, but she says she has to go; she understands, but she has to go. I almost decide to bail too, but I don't. I just don't. I go back into the bar, get cleaned up in the bathroom, and do four giant bumps.

The music is pounding. Ted is still right up front, but so is everyone else now. The place can only hold some fifty people, but all fifty are there, and all fifty are up and grooving. I go back to my spot at the side of the bar, knock back two Jägers, and as I watch and listen, I drink Smithwick's after Smithwick's after Smithwick's until the bar begins to swirl around me and everybody disappears into a smear of sound and motion and into one another we are lifted up off the floor and fed into a twister of sound and motion everything is compressed we are squeezed together then pushed through a tube at the end of which each of us one by one is spit out into oblivion.

25

later that night, at the Valley-Hi

Swanson, the Steamer, and Old George are in Swanson's room. They are standing close together at the foot of the bed. Swanson is staring obliquely at Old George. Swanson is ripped; he is unstable. He is hostile; he is deranged.

"He's fucking with you, dude," the Steamer says. "He is totally fucking with you."

"Are you fucking with me? Are you seriously fucking with me? Don't you fuck with me, old man. I am a philosopher, goddamnit. I don't shovel fucking mud, okay. That's your fucking job."

"What? Look," Old George says, "I really don't know what you guys are talking about, and I don't understand what's happening here. I know you're a philosopher, Eric, and I'm not fucking with you about shoveling mud or anything else, and I have no idea why you would think or say that I was. It's like you just pulled the idea out of thin air, that you just made it up. Look, maybe you're hallucinating or something, Eric. Maybe you're just high and confused."

"Oh, he is definitely fucking with you now, Socrates," the Steamer says. "He's saying you don't know what you're talking about, man. He's saying you're out of your mind."

"What! You think I don't know what I'm talking about? You think I'm just making this shit up? That I'm out of my mind? Fuck! Fuck you, old man! I'm the fucking philosopher here! I know what I heard and I know what the fuck I'm talking about!"

"No, wait, whoa, Eric, please, slow down. Don't listen to this..."

The Steamer runs Old George against the wall and pins him there. He points with his eyes to the hunting knife on Old George's belt. "Take it," he says.

Swanson takes the hunting knife off of Old George's belt and holds it up to Old George's neck right up to his neck in weird fury it shakes there at his neck and in Swanson two voices commence with the shaking over and over they whisper and sing in fugue "You're junk" says his father's the Steamer's says "Do it" "You're junk Do it Do it You're Junk Do it Do it You're Junk Do it..." he's shaking he's shaking the knife at Old George's neck he's shaking the knife at Old George's neck the Steamer wraps his hand around Swanson's "Do it You're junk" Swanson hears and possessed he feels the power and they do it.

Swanson pulls out the knife. He drops it onto the bed. Old George falls to the floor. He holds his neck. Blood is going everywhere. He moans and gurgles. Swanson looks around. The Steamer is gone.

Swanson picks up the phone and calls the Steamer. No answer. He stands there.

He goes to the door. He opens it and looks up and down the hall.

He takes Old George's arms and drags him down the hall. He grabs a shovel from the utility closet. He takes the shovel out to campsite number six and leans it against a tree.

He goes back inside. Old George is sitting up. He says,

"Eric." Swanson takes his arms and drags him outside, to campsite number six. He lays him in the snow.

He digs through snow and ice and dirt. He digs a shallow grave. He's thinking all the time, *This is what I have to do, this is what I have to do, this is what I have to do, this is what I have to do...*

He rolls Old George into the hole. Old George reaches his arm up toward him. He throws dirt on Od George. *This is what I have to do.* He covers him with dirt and ice and snow.

He goes back inside the Valley-Hi. He has blood all over him. He goes back to his room. There's blood everywhere. Old George had fallen on top of his backpack. There's blood all over it, all in it, all over his stuff, all over his clothes.

He goes down the hall to Old George's camping closet. He grabs a shirt, pants, socks, boots, gloves, a jacket.

He goes back to his room and takes a shower. He puts on all Old George's clothes.

He take his money and his ID and credit cards and anything with his name on it out of his wallet and puts it in his pocket. He puts his wallet and everything else that is his: clothes, keys, books, everything – into his backpack. He puts old George's hunting knife into his backpack.

He goes down the hall to the utility closet and gets a large garbage bag. He puts his backpack into the garbage bag.

He goes to the office. He opens the safe and takes all the money and puts it in his pocket.

He goes back to his room. He stands there. There's blood everywhere. He picks up the phone and calls the Steamer. No answer. He looks around. There's nothing of his left.

He takes the garbage bag and leaves the Valley-Hi. He crosses the parking lot. He crosses the highway. He takes the ID and credit card pieces out of his pocket and puts them in a garbage can outside McDonald's. He walks along the highway, up toward Mary Jane.

He stops along the way and throws Old George's knife into the woods.

There's a large garbage bin near the Mary Jane parking lot. He throws the garbage bag up into the bin and sees in the sky the earliest blue of dawn.

He falls against the bin. He slides down the bin into the snow. He rests.

26

late summer 1999

I woke up to the sound of a shovel scraping across concrete just outside my window. A wave of nausea hit me so intense, it was all I could do to stumble to the bathroom and throw up into the tub. I caught my breath, got up off the floor, dumped the toothbrush out of my toothbrush holder cup, and like a lunatic gobbled down five or six cups of pasty water, water spilling over my face and neck and chest. I hobbled back to bed and got under the covers as fucking Old George shoveled and swept the mud from the sidewalk right outside my window, doing my job, the one I had promised him I would do.

It was late afternoon when I came to again. The light seeping around the curtain was deeper, falling. I stared at it for a minute. I moved a leg, an arm. Slowly I pushed myself up and sat on the edge of the bed.

I shuffled over to the sink and drank several more cups of water. The smell of vomit in the tub was overwhelming. I put my pants on and went down to the janitor's closet.

I cleaned the tub and took a shower.

I left the Valley-Hi and walked down the street to McDonald's. I needed to eat. It was close by. I felt confident that I wouldn't see anyone I knew there; only tourists ate at McDonald's. I darted across the highway and slipped inside.

I sat down in the corner with a quarter-pounder, fries, and a coke. The food was yellow, the drink was black, but it was all good. I ordered a second quarter-pounder.

I returned to the Valley–Hi, went to the manager's office, grabbed a sleeping bag and a flashlight out of Old George's camping closet, and headed out back to campsite number six. Before making a fire, I threw out my sleeping bag and just lay down on it for a while, looking up through the trees at the twilighting sky, the cool pink strips of cloud glowing beneath an ever-deepening cobalt blue dome.

"I'll make it up to you, George," I said. I'm leaving tomorrow, but I'll make it up to you somehow.

27

The birds tweeped and twirped and cheeped and chirped beside the babbling brook, and it was, for a moment, as if nothing had ever happened and everything going forward was going to be brand new.

I rolled inside my sleeping bag from my side onto my back and looked straight up through the towering pines behind the Valley-Hi. In the space between the branches, set off in relief against the backdrop of the whitening sky, I saw an eagle fly, like an augury. I knew, however, that the bird up above may not have been an eagle and that whatever kind of bird it was, an augury, in this world, most likely it was not.

As I lay there, the cats began to approach me from all sides. One easily cleared the brook; others appeared from behind the trunks of trees; still others, out of nowhere.

"I'm awake," I said.

I stood up and stretched. I gathered my sleeping bag into my arms. Several cats rammed their heads into my ankles and dragged the lengths of their bodies along my calves.

"All right, all right." I slipped my feet into my boots. "No need to get sexy."

I counted seven cats. What would happen if that number increased? How many cats could be accommodated?

I returned to the motel. They followed me, jogging and

bouncing and meowing. We all went up the steps onto the deck behind the office. I looked for the key; the cats made circles below me. I popped open the door; they all assumed they were to come right in, but I used my foot and the bottom of the sleeping bag to block them. I closed the door in their faces.

I came back out and shook the large bag of food; they went into a chorus of circular celebrations and demands. I poured the pellets into the two large bowls; they raced to them, drawn like high-powered magnets. They jammed together, they crouched, eating, their mouths in the bowls, right next to one another, no fighting.

I went inside, sat down at the desk in the office, and checked the books. There was no one scheduled to check-in that day, or for the next several days, and there was no one currently checked-in.

I leaned back, twisted around in the old chair, and stared out the window into the colonnade of pines. I decided I was going to close up the motel for the rest of the day and head up mountain, myself, up Parry Peak. I had plenty of time to get up to Vista Point and back before catching the seven o'clock bus to Denver International.

But first, I did a few chores. I put a message on the telephone answering system, flipped the sign on the door and headed out into the campsite to collect fees from any campers that might have come in over night. But there were none. So I went and placed the "Camping Honor Box" sign and the camping honor box on the pole at the entrance to the campground and headed off to empty all the garbage bins.

I returned to the office and had breakfast: peanut butter, banana, water; I grabbed a couple granola bars from the cupboard and filled up a large plastic water bottle; I left a *note for Old George apologizing about the walkway, promising to make it up to him, and telling him I'd be sure to stop by before I left town. And I decided to call Nico.*

"Nico," I said, "It's Eric."

Immediately she called me an asshole, but I convinced her to stay on the line.

"Nico, I'm calling to apologize. No one deserves to be treated the way I treated you, and I am very, very sorry."

She didn't say anything. She was crying.

"Nico. Listen. What I did was wrong, and I feel terrible about it, okay. I just thought you should hear that from me."

"You were avoiding me."

"No, no. I just...it was just a typical asshole-guy thing to do."

There was a long pause.

"Nico."

"Well," she said quietly, "Do you want to come over to my place now?"

"No, no, Nico. I'm sorry," I said. "It's just not like that."

28

I headed through the campground on the footpath that leads from the Valley-Hi to the base of the Parry Peak. It was cool, breezy, and sunny. I felt free and clean. This was my last day in Winter Park; tonight, I was off to Texas.

I was lucky, lucky to be alive and lucky to have found a way out of Winter Park. Philosophy had delivered me. Getting accepted to the program at Rice was a miracle. Their letter was the last to arrive; in fact, because I had been waitlisted, it wasn't until July that I received it. All prior - from Berkeley, Yale, Vanderbilt, NYU, Washington, Emory, Virginia - were rejections.

I was aware that philosophy is the quintessential ivory tower - or, as a man on a chairlift once put it to me, "an irrelevant, self-perpetuating microcosm" - and I knew that its rigors might not jibe well with my wilder, more artistic side. But what was any of that to me now? For some three hours I climbed, peacefully; everything was embraced by the loving arms of absolute value. For some three hours, I was free.

29

I topped the ridge at Vista Point and rested a minute, but before I could catch my breath a frigid current of air swept over me. I turned around. A massive bank of black cloud was rolling over the valley, over the mountains, over me. It rolled between the earth and sun like an errant planet. The temperature plummeted from crisp to below freezing almost instantly. Dark walls of precipitation hung like lead curtains beneath the clouds. Everything turned icy grey.

I started back down the trail. The wind, like cold scissors, was cutting into my pants and slicing across my neck and chest. I stopped, zipped up my windbreaker, looped the water bottle back onto my belt, and set off again, padding my way down the steep trail.

It started to snow. The first flakes were small and light and barely visible. Within minutes they were coming down by the billions, large, thick, and close together. There were no trees, no dark structures, nothing on either side of me to guide me down the corridor of the trail, but I could make out the tree line below.

I reached the tree line and paused. The canopy was slowing the accumulation of snow on the trail. The trees cut the wind as well. But the amount of daylight remaining had been cut in half. I went on.

I came off the main slope onto flatter terrain cold and

exhausted. The trailhead was still an hour plus. Mechanically, I pushed on, my eyes fixed on the ground in front of me, my body disintegrating in thick mountain twilight.

I stopped.

My eyes were drawn from the ground slowly upward, along its legs, over its chest, up its neck to its head and antlers, which stretched out wide and high above him like two huge petrified wooden hands. There was no sound except the evacuation of his breath. It came out of his nostrils in two long white shoots. His right eye, shiny-black, abysmal, like some de-bagged testicle, stared down at me. The white crescent above it thickened. His knees buckled and he fell toward me. I collapsed into a ball on the ground.

30

But there was nothing. Nothing more. Nothing happened.

Keeping my head bowed, I raised myself up on my elbows and knees. I picked my left knee up out of the snow and moved it back a few inches. I did the same with my right, and, watching where I was going through my legs, slowly crawled backwards up the trail. I angled into the trees to my left and looked up. The moose was still standing in the middle of the trail staring at me. I backed up some more, until I could barely make him out. I sat against a tree.

It was risky to portage around him and try to hook back up with the trail. The trail is circuitous, and with the snow and the failing light, there was a good chance I'd never find it again. The only other choice I had was to forget the trail altogether and head south, through the woods, toward the highway, which couldn't have been far, but I didn't really know. I had about half an hour, maybe, of twilight left. I had to decide. I went south.

I tromped through the trees and snow. The light faded, but before it got dark, I heard running water. It had to be the Fraser River. This was good. It runs roughly parallel to the highway and flows west right into town along with it. I approached it, but its banks were cluttered and crowded with trees and brush. Passage near its banks was impossible.

I pulled back and tried to follow it by ear.

But twilight gave way to darkness, and I lost the river, and with all the snow and no moon, I was, for all practical purposes, blind, so at the foot of an incline, I stopped and I listened to the tiny clicks of a billion snowflakes landing all around me.

I took a step to go – I was freezing, I had to go – but something caught my attention, like a tone or a note, cutting through the snow. I stood still. It was getting louder. It was getting louder and louder. Yes, and with those distinctive grating and humming noises, there was no doubt now. It was a snowplow.

The roar of the engine was coming down toward me from the left. I tried to climb up to it, but the incline was too steep and slick with snow. The plow was headed straight for me. It scraped and screamed by just overhead. A heavy cape of wet snow crashed over me.

I shook it off and hopped and tromped my way with new energy west along the incline, following the sound of the plow. The incline flattened out some. I got on my hands and knees, scrambled up it, and rolled out onto the shoulder of the highway.

31

spring break 2000

"Holy fucking shit! Hey! Hey man! Are you okay?" I open my eyes. Snow. It's dark out. Someone kneels beside me. "Socrates! Jesus Christ! Are you all right?" It's Big Dave.

I raise my head up off the snow. "What? Why? What happened?"

"Dude, you're lying face down in the snow near Mary Jane!"

"Oh. Shit." He helps me roll over onto my back.

"Yeah, man. What the fuck?"

I put my hand to my head. I've got gloves on. They're not mine. "I don't know. I don't know."

"Well are you all right? Are you hurt?"

I get up on my elbows. We're behind a large garbage bin. Big Dave helps me sit up all the way. "I'm sore, but I think...I think I'm all right."

Big Dave shakes his head. "Wow, man. I thought you were dead. I thought you were a dead man. What happened to you? What the hell are you doing out here?"

My jacket, my pants, my shirt: none of them is mine. "God. What the fuck," I whisper. I reach for my wallet my keys, no wallet no keys, but there's something, paper. I pull it out. Money. I put it back.

"What? What, man? What is it?"

"Nothing. It's just, I..." I look at my boots. They're Old George's, from his camping closet. "Can we get in the car?"

"Yeah, yeah," he says. "If you're sure you're not hurt. Here, come here."

Big Dave helps me to my feet and into the car. He turns it on and gets the heat going. We sit there a minute. He keeps looking over at me. "Man, I'm glad I saw you. From Ted's door, I could just make you out lying back there. Do you think you need to see a doctor? Maybe go to the emergency room?"

"No."

"You want to go up to Ted's? It's right here? I was just..."

"No, no."

"You're good then? You want to go?"

I nod. "Yeah, I want to go. Let's go."

"All right." He turns the headlights on, puts the car in gear, and pulls out of the parking lot onto the highway heading back toward Winter Park.

"So, how long do you think you were out there? What the hell were you doing?"

I stare out the windshield. "I don't know. The last thing I remember...is watching that band, Weirdo, at the No Holds."

"Dude! That was last night!"

I inhale.

"God, you must've been absolutely fucking hammered!"

We pass the Valley-Hi, and it all comes back. I start coughing. I gag.

"You okay?"

"Holy shit." I gag again. "I gotta go, man. I gotta go. I got to get the fuck out of here right now. What time is it?"

"6:54, dude," Big Dave says pointing to the green lights on the dashboard.

"Oh fuck! Right now. I gotta get to the bus station, right now. The last one's at seven. I got a plane out of Denver at eleven."

"You sure? What about your backpack? Where's your backpack?"

"No, no, man. Fuck my backpack. Just take me to the goddamn bus station, now...please!"

"All right, all right. Whatever you say, brother. Whatever you say."

32

I run into the restroom in the bus station. I lock myself in a stall and throw up. I sit back against the wall. I throw up again. They call the Denver International bus. I stay where I am.

When I come out, it's 7:30pm. I have to go. I have to go somewhere. Now.

I see that the last bus of the night is an 8:00pm to Odessa, Texas.

I buy a ticket and go back into the restroom to hide before it's called.

I decide that I will go to Odessa and kill myself.

WINTER PARK

Part 2

Nat Stobbs
aka Harris Birdsong

&

Eric Swanson
aka Wayne Floyd

WINTER PARK

33

end spring break 2000

The bus stops at the station in Odessa Odessa Odessa Texas everything's flat it's flat and yellow and they ain't no trees nowhere nowhere just brown shrubs I get off the bus it's hot I walk out into a field of shrubs I kick one it holds onto the toe of my boot I yank my boot out of the shrub I walk back back across the parking lot.

There's a girl standing outside the station I had a girl a girlfriend Lilah back at home Lilah.

"What was it? What'd you see out there?" she says.

"Don't, don't go out there," I tell her.

"Why? What was it, a snake? Did you see a snake?" She blows cigarette smoke out the side of her mouth up up into the air.

"No, no snake. It was a shrub. Look, look at this." I hold out the toe of my boot. "See all them little holes?"

"Mm, yeah."

I put down my boot. "Take care." I go into the station.

"Mr. Birdsong? Harris Birdsong?" says a man with a clipboard Nat said daddy over the phone from home I was in that hotel room in Jackson listen to me now when you get off the bus in Odessa momma says this namby-pamby sounding white fellow name Chip Geener he gonna meet you he gonna come up to you but this is very important he ain't gonna call you Nat Stobbs he gonna call you by another name he gonna call you Harris Birdsong Harris Birdsong okay that's what he's going to call you Harris Birdsong gonna be your Dude Ranch name your cowboy name your only name okay? "Yes, yes," I say, "I am Harris Birdsong."

"Fantastic." He writes on his clipboard and don't *never* tell nobody who you really are or where you're from you hear me? Daddy said *never*. "I'm Chip Geener, the coordinator for the trip over today. It's great to have you. Now, if you'll just follow me over yonder I'll…" He takes a few steps I stay where I am he turns around and comes back. "First we're going to pair you up with your dude-brother then we're all going to climb aboard Old Myrtle and ramble on out to Dude Ranch."

On his shirt on the chest on his shirt it says *Dude* Ranch and there's a little picture of man man with a rake in his hand.

"But I ain't got no brother," I tell him I say, "and, and a dude ranch is a vacation resort offering outdoor activities that is or resembles a typical western ranch, but, but a dude is a man or boy and a ranch is a large farm devoted to keeping a single species of animal."

"I am sorry. I should've been clearer. Dude Ranch is on the dude-brother system, Mr. Birdsong. That means you're paired, while you're at the Ranch, with somebody we think you'll be compatible with, and then y'all work together, everyday. It's modeled after the Butch Cassidy and Sundance Kid dude-brotherhood. But, if you just can't get along, you can petition the vice-warden for a change." He stops talking he starts talking. "It's a common and perfectly understandable misconception that Dude Ranch is for men only, when actually, well it depends, but most of the time it's about an even split men to women. The confusion comes from the fact that Dude, as you say, usually means a man, but in this case Dude is the last name of the family that runs the Ranch. In fact, our current warden is a woman, Warden Judy Dude. She's fifth generation Dude...anyway, listen, Mr. Birdsong, I hate to...but does that answer your questions? Because I got a strict itinerary to keep."

"Yes, yes, Mr. Geener, okay, yes."

Chip Geener walks toward a group of people standing and sitting and standing and sitting against the wall on the other side side of the station I follow him I'm following him I say, "Who who's Old Myrtle?"

He turns around he keeps walking. "School bus. Big yellow school bus. Been toting Dude Ranchers around for over thirty years."

We come up on the group of people and Chip Chip Geener says, "Okay, Floyd, Wayne." They look at Chip Geener. "Floyd? No? Anyone seen Mr. Floyd or know where he is?" They ain't seen Floyd Wayne. "Anyone talked to Mr. Floyd in the last ten minutes?"

Chip Geener turns to me. "All right, I know he's here." He looks around he sees a man the man's sitting on the floor in the corner in the corner the man is sitting his head is down on his arms. "Ah. There he is. It's interesting, before I introduce you I'll tell you, Mr. Floyd just joined us today. I found him sleeping on the floor here in the station early this morning. He was a little...lost, but I explained to him about Dude Ranch and lo and behold, he was game. So I rang up the Vice Warden, Rudy Dude, Warden Judy's brother, and he said, 'Of course, bring him on, and put him with that

Birdsong fellow'." He touches me with his clipboard he smiles. "You see, it was a happy development for us because when we were contacted the other day by your sponsor, about you, we took you, but you were a late addition too, which meant, until this morning anyway, you were the odd man, you hadn't been assigned a dude-brother yet."

"Oh, okay, okay," I say.

"You'll see. Having a dude-brother is crucial to a successful experience at the Ranch. Some people don't think so at first, but they always change their minds by the end." He takes a few steps he stops. "Of course, you know, Dude Ranch operates under strict anonymity when it comes to you all, but I can't believe it'll do any harm to tell you this too. Mr. Floyd says he's taking a break from his studies right now to, work on some things, but apparently," he holds up his clipboard between us he whispers, "Mr. Floyd is a philosopher."

34

"Mr. Floyd?" Chip Geener says. "Mr. Floyd, dude, I want to introduce you to Harris Birdsong, your dude-brother." Chip Geener turns to me. "You don't have to, but we like it if you call your dude-brother, dude. We like to think of everyone at the Ranch as part of the Dude family." He turns back to Mr. Floyd Mr. Floyd has not moved. "Mr. Floyd," he says.

"Is Mr. Floyd sick, Mr. Geener?" I say. "He don't look so good."

Chip Geener kneels down and touches he touches Mr. Floyd on the shoulder Mr. Floyd says, "What? What do you want now?" to the floor between his legs.

"I am sorry to bother you, Mr. Floyd. I just wanted you to meet someone special."

"No. Go away."

Chip Geener stands up. "All right. Well. I'll leave y'all to it. But in about, oh fifteen-twenty minutes, listen up for my whistle." He put his fingers together up near his mouth his head goes back it goes down he's gonna put his fingers in his mouth he doesn't. "That'll be the signal to gather over at gate ten over yonder, okay?"

"Yes, yes, all right."

"It's a pleasure to have you with us, Mr. Birdsong."

We shake hands he walks he walks away I sit down on

the floor next to Mr. Floyd.

"Namby, namby-pamby," I say.

Mr. Floyd laughs he starts coughing he chokes I hit his back he rolls his head side-to-side on his arms. "No, stop, I'm fine, I'm fine."

"I'm sorry, Mr. Floyd. Can I help you?"

"No, and don't be sorry, and don't be feeling sorry for me. Feeling sorry for people is arrogant and disrespectful. And it's mamby-pamby. Mamby, with an m."

"No, no Mr. Floyd, that's not what The Book says. The Book says namby with a n, and I ain't never, I ain't never heard that about feeling sorry for people, no, no I ain't."

"Look, if you feel sorry for someone," he's still talking to the floor, "you think that person is pitiful, and pathetic, and that you're in a better, higher place than he is." He coughs. "That is arrogance. You look down on his position in relation to yours, and that is disrespectful."

"The Book says arrogance is a strong feeling of proud self-importance that is expressed by treating other people with contempt or disregard."

"Exactly." He coughs some more. "Feeling sorry for someone exposes your pride and your contempt of others. And what is this *book* you keep referring to, some kind of dictionary?"

"A dictionary is a reference book that contains words listed in alphabetical order and gives explanations of their meanings, often with additional information about grammar, pronunciation, and etymology. The Book is the dictionary, it is the dictionary, but The Book says The Book on the front of it, in wood, in wood. Daddy made a cover for it. It says The Book in wood. It does not, not say the dictionary on the front of it in wood. I have memorized The

Book. The first word in The Book is A, and the last word in The Book is ZZZ, yes it is."

He turns his head sideways his face is green. "No. There's no way, man."

"There's no way *dude*, dude, Mr. Floyd."

"All right, please stop calling me mister, and it's not *the* dictionary, it's a dictionary because there are hundreds of different dictionaries, and there is absolutely no way that you have one memorized."

"Well, well, you can ask me any word you want to, Floyd, ask me any word you want to, I'll tell you what it is."

"Bullshit."

"No, no, bullshit ain't in there, Floyd. It ain't in there because it's naughty."

"Come on, man."

"Come on, *dude.*"

He turns his face back toward the floor. "All right. Dubious. What's the definition of dubious?"

"Uncertain about an outcome or conclusion. Likely to be dishonest, untrustworthy, or morally worrisome in some way. Of...uncertain quality, intention, or appropriateness."

"Liar."

"Somebody who tells lies."

"Lies."

"False statements made deliberately, and a false impression created deliberately."

"Supercilious."

"Super...full of contempt and arrogance."

"Phenomenology."

"In philosophy, the science or study of phenomena, things as they are perceived, as opposed to the study of being, the nature of things as they are. The philosophical investigation and description of conscious experience in all its varieties without reference to the question of whether what is experienced is objectively real."

"All right."

"Generally good, satisfactory, or..."

"No, no, man, *dude.* That's good, that's enough, thank you. I am impressed." He turns his head back toward me. "How in the hell did you manage that?"

"Momma says it's on account of my fits."

"What, like epilepsy?"

"Epilepsy, epilepsy." The song the song that is the definition of epilepsy epilepsy is a medical disorder involving episodes of abnormal electrical discharge in the brain and characterized by periodic sudden loss or impairment of consciousness, often accompanied by convulsions. "I don't know...that sounds right, but they was always just fits, just fits to us. I didn't go to school, no, didn't go, didn't go to school with all the other kids. I stayed home, stayed home and did lessons in The Book, I did lessons in the morning with momma in The Book. I worked outside on the farm with daddy, on the farm with daddy in the afternoon. Momma says The Book's got everything in it, everything in it. We went through it in the mornings, over and over and over and over. Then one day, after a real bad fit, after a real bad fit I woke up and had all the words and definitions, all the words and definitions in my head, in my head, and all the definitions had turned into little songs in my head, all of them different, all of them different little songs, and that's the way I know them now, now they are a whole bunch of different little songs in my head."

"You're a synaesthete, then."

"Synes...I don't...do you mean synesthesia?"

"Yeah, synesthesia."

"Synesthesia is the evocation of one kind of sense impression when another is stimulated, for example, the sensation of color when sound is heard."

"Yeah, so when you think of a definition, it's not just in language, it's also in music."

"Yes, that's right, that's right."

"But so, does it bother you? I mean, is it always on?"

"No, no, it ain't always on, it ain't always singing like it or not, like it or not, but The Book is handy, it's handy, handy all the time. If somebody, somebody asks me a word, or if I, I want to look a word up, it sings, that's when it sings."

"So when I'm talking, there aren't a million little songs playing at the same time?"

"No, no."

Chip Geener whistles.

35

A whole bunch of us go out the gate out the gate into the parking lot Old Myrtle's in the parking lot Old Myrtle's a school bus a yellow school bus it says school bus on it in the station Chip Geener said Old Myrtle's in the parking lot and that's where Old Myrtle is there are a lot of kids mostly white kids some white girls – Lilah – there's a man taking bags from people throwing them into the back of the bus everybody's white except me everybody's white except me and the man throwing bags into the back of the bus me and Floyd ain't got no bags we just climb on the bus Floyd falls backwards on the steps I catch him I push him up we go down the aisle halfway halfway down Floyd drops onto a bench he drops onto a bench his head his head falls against the window I sit next to him.

"I'll get some water, Floyd, some water, Floyd, and a sandwich. They have water and a sandwich up there, Floyd, in that big white cooler. I'll get, I can..."

"No." Floyd shakes his head.

The back door shuts everybody's sitting on the bus no one else is coming on the bus or walking in the aisle everyone is talking the man who was throwing the bags into the back of the bus climbs onto the bus he starts the engine Chip Geener stands up Chip Geener whistles.

"Okay everybody. Can I have your attention, please.

Welcome! Welcome back from spring break, welcome all new counsellors and ranch hands, and welcome aboard Old Myrtle. Our ride this afternoon will take us about three hours. Use that time to chat with your fellow Dudes and Dudettes. We got plenty of food and drink up here in the cooler. It is hot and, as you can see, the only a/c Old Myrt's got is au naturale, so leave your windows down and stay hydrated. If you need to pee, well you should have done that already, but we will be making one pit stop at a rest area near Pecos, just before we head south toward the Davis Mountains and Dude Ranch. If it's an emergency, and *only* if it's an emergency, use a Gatorade bottle, but if you do, please, *please* cap the bottle, remove it from the bus at your first opportunity, and dispose of it properly. All right. If you have any other questions, come on up at any time. Either me or Juan will be happy to answer them. We love the area and we love talking about it. And hey, what am I doing? Let's put our hands together for Old Myrt's one and only driver for what, the last fifteen years? Yeah." Chip Geener claps. "Juan, Juan Flores, everybody. Come on." I clap nobody else claps nobody else claps. "All right. Oh, and I should mention. The forecast calls for some Texas-size storms down near ranch country, maybe even some hail, you never know, so buckle up, could get bumpy." He looks at Juan. "Okay. Well, if that's it, then, without further ado I say, let's hit the road!"

We're going we're going to go we're going Floyd's asleep.

We go the bus goes out of the station into the street the bus is loud it's bumpy the streets are bumpy the bus is bumpy and the hot wind comes into the bus in Odessa Odessa out the window of the bus is short flat flat boxes yellow dusty boxes the bus goes up onto the ramp slowly it's loud the windows shake the more they shake the more the bus goes up onto the ramp the bus roars up the ramp onto the highway on the highway it goes west loudly.

We drive and drive we drive a long time it's all yellow yellow everywhere yellow except them shrubs them shrubs and and these big bird big bird machines go up and down up and down.

A man with a white afro is sitting in front front of me I lean forward I say, "Could, could you tell me? What, what are those things out there, going up and down?"

He turns around I sit back it ain't just his hair he's white he's white all over.

"What's that, dude? Oh, you mean, like, the oil wells? Those are oil wells. Haven't you ever seen oil wells before?"

I shake my head I can almost see through him his eyes are pink. "No, no, I reckon I ain't."

"That's cool. What's your name, dude?"

"It's Harris. Birdsong. It's Harris Birdsong."

"I'm Cosmic." He puts his white white hand over the back of the seat at me I reach up and take it it's light and soft and loose.

"Cosmic, cosmic, wow, really?"

"Exactly, but like, not really." He laughs. "My last name *is* Wow, but I spell it 'W' 'a' 'u'. It's like, Hawaiian, and really is not part of it. Cosmic's my first name. It's like, a nickname for Charles. I am, therefore, Charles Cosmic Wau, the albino. But you can call me 'Cosmic'."

"You, you got to...you made up your own name name, Cosmic?"

"Yeah. Well they like, gave me one, but I petitioned for a change. So what up with him? Is he your dude-brother?"

"Yes, yes. That's Floyd, that's Mr. Floyd, Wayne. He's

tired I, I reckon."

"My dude-brother's right up there, with the hat over his face. His name's Monty Jolly. We're ranch hands. Are you a ranch hand or an instructor? You're not, like, an instructor are you?"

"I, I don't know..."

"Well, at Dude Ranch, they got students, and instructors, and then they got ranch hands, and like, if you don't know if you're a instructor or not, like, you're not an instructor. Instructor's like a job. You like, train for it and get paid. And you're too old to be a student, dude. Therefore, you are a ranch hand. Jolly and I are ranch hands too. And if he's your dude-brother, Floyd's a ranch hand too. That might be all the ranch hands, not including the girls. So how come you don't know what you are?"

"I, I don't know, Cosmic. My daddy, he, he said I was going to a ranch to be a cowboy and ride horses."

He laughs. "That's funny. But seriously, like, what did you do?"

"What did I...do?"

"You don't have to say, of course, but I ask because, for ranch hands, Dude Ranch is like, work camp. It's like, doing time for something bad you did, but it's not like, part of the state, like, penalty system or whatever. You don't like, get sent here by a court or a judge or something. A lot of times like, your family sends you. Sometimes people just like, send themselves, and you stay here until you graduate." He does something with his fingers he makes hooks with his fingers over the back of the seat he puts them away. "Or, in other words, when they say you're fit for release. This is like, my second time, for drugs. That's how come I know so much about it. But like, it isn't that bad, dude. I was upset the first time they sent me, but I was like, totally willing to go this time. It can be a really...personal experience, you know? Like, a really good place to hide out from the world and like, get clear, you know. Yeah." His head goes it goes up and down up and down.

"I, I had a girlfriend, Lilah, Lilah, back at home. She was white, and everyone in town, the white folks in town was upset, and I had to go to Jackson and I had to change my name then I had to come here."

Chip Geener whistles. "Okay people. We're pulling into the rest stop at Pecos. Everybody do their business and be back on the bus in fifteen minutes, no longer."

"Oh, thank god, dude," Cosmic says, "I have like, had to pee ever since we left."

"Chip Geener said pee, pee before, back, back there at the station, dude."

"Yeah, I know."

36

I'm getting off I'm getting off the bus I step down one foot down off the bus onto into onto the parking lot but I pick my foot back up and turn around I turn around and go back up back up the steps up the steps people go around people go around pushing down I push back up up the aisle back up to Floyd I get to Floyd but Floyd's still asleep I sit I wait for Floyd to wake up.

Cosmic's hair Cosmic's head Cosmic comes back Cosmic gets on Cosmic stops and sits up with his dude-brother Monty Jolly Chip Geener stands up and counts Chip Chip Geener counts everybody on the bus bus.

"Okay," Chip Geener says. "Now, everybody. Off to the south, to our left, coming over the mountains, is the weather I was telling you about, and in just a few minutes, we are going to head directly into it." Everyone goes everyone goes over to the left side my side of the bus bus to look to see the sky off in the distance the sky is filled with green cloud and black cloud and up up in the sky there are silver strings of lightening flashing flashing up and down and sideways up and down and sideways in it. "I talked to the ranger inside here, and though there have been no reports of tornado, it has been reported that the storm is packing hail. You can rest assured, however, that Juan has a whole heck of a lot of experience with this sort of thing, so there is nothing to be concerned about. In fact, think of it as a treat, a great big Texas-sized treat. Welcome to Texas!" Chip Geener sits down.

We drive and drive a man in a hat it's a black cowboy hat it's tipped back on his head he takes out a guitar and goes up and down telling up and down telling tells everyone on the bus to get up and go back back to the back back to sing sing songs with him and a girl in the back in the back back of the bus and a girl Lilah a girl is behind him coming with him with his guitar he comes up to us me and Floyd.

"Howdy boys," he says. "Name's David Hill. This is my sister, Rachel." Lilah he holds up her hand with his hand. "And this here's Roberta." He holds up his guitar in his hand with his other hand. "So what do you say? Let Jesus be your chaperon on this blessed day? Praise him in song as we head into the storm?"

I shake my head I look at Floyd he opens his eyes a little he closes his eyes again.

"No, no thank you," I say, "no thank you."

"Seriously?" David Hill says. "Guys, come on. Let's get together on this. In the back. On the double."

Floyd opens his eyes he leans forward he says, "Hey. Fuckin' no way, man, *dude*. Now fuck off." Floyd then lets lets his body fall forward his head hits the seat his head stays on the seat he rests his head on the back of the seat in front in front of us.

David Hill stands straight up he stares at us. "Drug addicts and sinners. Y'all always got to make it harder for everybody else, don't you." He looks down down the aisle he picks up his guitar in his arms in his hands he hits it and sings, "Michael!" but nobody nobody claps or says anything he hits it again. "Michael! Oh come on, people! In the back, right now, Michael row your boat ashore!"

"Hey Floyd. Hey Floyd, I was talking to the man, the man who was sitting right right here before. He, his name was is Cosmic. He said we're fixing to, that me and you are fixing to work, to go to work at work camp out here, Floyd. Are we going to work out here? My daddy told me I'm going to be a cowboy and ride horses, Floyd.

"Cosmic said we ain't students or instructors. He said we're ranch hands we're ranch hands so we must of we must of done something bad back at home. He said we come out here to be punished. My daddy didn't say nothing about being punished. I had a white girlfriend, but I...did, did you do something bad back at home, Floyd?"

Floyd is shivering.

"Hey, hey Floyd! What, what is it? What's the matter?"

David Hill and Rachel start to sing they sing the sun goes away it goes away cold cold air fills the bus.

"Buckle up!" Chip Geener shouts Floyd's body bolts upright his head hits the window and he sings he sings out, "Ope, ope, ope ope, woop-woop-woop-woop-woop-woop-woop-woop!" his chin pushes down on his chest. "What, Floyd, what? What is it, what is it?" He shakes shakes his eyes are shaking open and shaking watching something not something a string of spit and blood blood drops out of his mouth onto his shirt a stain fills his pants I stand up I hit my head I hit my head on the bar where the bags go the bags go I grab my fold over head over fall over grab and fall over head bees bees bees swarm are swarming that grows it becomes the sound of becoming stones striking a thousand stones striking the roof that becoming becomes the blaring of a million trains coming freight train horns blaring they're coming they're coming blaring blaring blaring I.

WINTER PARK

Part 3

Harris Birdsong

&

Wayne Floyd

WINTER PARK

37

summer session 2000

Consolidate is to combine separate items or scattered material into a single mass I make piles of rocks with a iron rake the end of the rake is a iron comb the teeth of the rake are iron the teeth of the rake are short it's hard to rake small rocks the handle of the rake is a iron pipe the pipe gets hot it hurts my hands I have to wear gloves.

Floyd pushes piles together he pushes piles together with a curved metal blade the blade goes on the front of his electrified chair Rudy Dude calls the blade a snowplow a snowplow is a vehicle or an implement that can be fixed to a vehicle used for clearing snow from roads or paths Floyd makes his own piles with the snowplow too it works better when he pushes piles together.

I put the rocks into the back of Rudy Dude's pickup truck I put them in the back back with a shovel and my hands Rudy Dude drives over to the mountain of rocks behind the hayloft me and Floyd walk and drive we walk and drive I throw the rocks out Floyd goes around the edge of the mountain with his snowplow Floyd makes sure no rocks get loose Floyd cleans up.

Floyd can't move he can't move at all except his hands

and fingers and eyes he can't talk that's why he's in the electrified chair Rudy Dude calls the chair Old Smokey it's big and black it's got big black tires on it and a motor Floyd hits the keyboards with his fingers to drive and talk he's got two keyboards one for each hand he talks out a machine in a box near his head.

We wear cowboy boots we wear jump suits the jump suits say 'DR' in brown letters on the back the boys' are blue the girls' are pink Rudy Dude makes Floyd wear a black beret a beret's a flat round soft hat with a tight-fitting headband it's not a sun hat there's a umbrella that goes on Floyd's Chair Jolly wears a brown cowboy hat Cosmic wears a sombrero a sombrero's a straw or felt hat with a very wide upturned brim he's white white all over I wear a yellow Cat Diesel baseball hat I found it outside in the dirt behind The Big House.

Rudy Dude comes in the main gate in his white pickup truck he drives over he leans out the window he goes in circles around us he wears shiny sunglasses he looks at the ground. "Don't mind me, goddammit," he says he's still going around. "Just keep consolidating those rocks, boys. Consolidate those rocks." He stops the truck. "René! How's my little philosopher today? You looking mighty cute in that hat, girlfriend. Most becoming. You just get back from gay Paris?"

Floyd types into his keyboards. "Fuck you. Take it off, Harris. Take it off me."

Rudy Dude laughs I go to take off Floyd's beret.

"All right, no. Stop right there, Birdsong. Don't you touch that hat now," Rudy Dude says I stop. "I know old René's your dude-brother and all, and I can appreciate your loyalty, but you leave that beanie right where it's at. René here's the only one gets to wear a hat for show, for style, and that's something special. Ain't that right, René?"

"Fuck," Floyd says.

"Aw," Rudy Dude says. "All right, all right. That's enough pillow-biting for one afternoon, now get back to work. I want this parking lot completely clear of rocks. Go on. Get to it." Rudy Dude is going to leave.

Floyd says, "Excuse me, but as I am sure you are aware, rocks are constitutive of this..."

"What? What is it, René? Constitutive of this what?"

Floyd drives over where I'm standing.

"Parking lot?" Rudy Dude laughs. "There ain't no point asking him." Rudy Dude laughs some more.

Floyd turns down his volume he says, "Oracle, what is a parking lot."

"It's, a parking lot is an open area of ground in which people can park their automobiles."

Rudy Dude stops laughing. "Hey. Is he talking to you?"

Floyd turns up his volume he drives back over to Rudy Dude he types. "A parking lot is an open area of ground in which people can park their automobiles, and because we have not considered or determined whether this area of ground is open we cannot yet say with certainty whether this particular area of ground is in fact a parking lot however since we are certain that rocks are constitutive of this particular area of ground we can also be certain that it is impossible practically speaking to, as you say, clear this ground completely of rocks. We will continue to uncover layer after layer of rocks because it's rocks all the way to the bottom."

Rudy Dude is looking down at Floyd. "Are you finished? Are you quite done, René, because I don't want to interrupt you, but if you are, I want to tell you a little story, okay? All right, look it. Say you got four pillars holding up a building and that one of them pillars is a retard. Guess where the structure fails? At the retard, and that's you, René, okay. You reduce the integrity of the ranch hand superstructure. It's a goddamned embarrassment to me, and the Ranch, and the great state of Texas to have a contorted idiot like you on this crew. Now get back to work. Clear this parking lot. Consolidate those goddamn rocks, boy," Rudy Dude says he drives away.

38

I go up the stairs to The Big House Floyd goes up the ramp I get to the doors first I say, "I win."

"What," Floyd says. "Don't say that. Why did you say that."

We go in. The first floor is Registration there's a long wood desk there's a big light it's made out of antlers it's hanging from the ceiling two old ladies work behind the desk they're back there I go over I push the button the elevator doors open Floyd goes in he runs into the back wall and has to back back up he does that a lot I get in I press three.

"Go slowly, Floyd," I say. "Go slowly."

Floyd types. "The accelerator mechanism is insensitive, Oracle. Isn't that obvious from observation alone. For an unmediated reader of essences, I am surprised at your remarkable lack of perceptual acuity. And since when were you disposed to offer personal advice."

The second floor is the country store you can take the stairs they got saddles lassoes boots hats spurs belts belt-buckles shirts jeans tents guns tiny cows tiny deer antlers antler lights rugs pens and they got cups.

The third floor's the infirmary me and Floyd stay in a room in the infirmary Doc Holiday and Nurse Cannary stay in the infirmary.

The warden stays on the fourth floor the fourth floor's the warden's quarters nobody can go up up there except the warden Rudy Dude can't go up there things go up there in the dumbwaiter a dumbwaiter's a small elevator used for moving food and tableware between the floors of a building it's right next to me and Floyd's room.

I've never seen the warden she never comes out Cosmic and Jolly were ranch hands before they say she used to come out a lot she used to come out for the rodeo Rudy Dude says she didn't come out for the last one the one in the spring she's gone crazy Rudy Dude says she might even be dead now she doesn't come out at all.

The doors open we go into the waiting room everything's old and white Nurse Cannary is young and pink she wears a white white dress and a little white hat the hat is a triangle she's young and pink and pretty she's sitting behind the desk she smiles.

"Hey boys."

"Hello," Floyd says.

"Hot out there today."

"Hot in here too," Floyd says he drives over to her desk.

Nurse Cannary blinks. "Oh. Why thank you, Wayne."

"My pleasure."

"You about ready to get cleaned up?"

"Ha ha. Yes," Floyd says.

Nurse Cannary looks at me. "He is such a card. All right. You two go on ahead. I'll be down in a minute. Oh, but let's not forget your vitamin, Wayne." She holds up a needle she sticks it into his arm. "Also, you two have a powwow with Doc Holiday in his office in about an hour." She nods towards the door to her right.

Floyd goes down the hall fast our room is all the way

down at the end it's at the back of the house it's the last room on the right all the rooms in the infirmary have names ours is called John Wayne's Room.

I go into the bathroom I take a shower I come out of the shower I come out of the bathroom Floyd goes into the bathroom he turns he turns his back's to the mirror he waits I put on a blue jumpsuit.

There's a knock on the door. "Guess who?"

I open the door Nurse Cannary's wearing her white robe and slippers and her little white hat I step back.

"Hi Harris. Floyd already in the...?"

We go into the bathroom Nurse Cannary takes off her robe she hangs it on the hook the hook's behind the door she's wearing her green swimsuit she turns around I point to my head.

"Oh dear. Thank you, Harris. She takes off her hat her hair's blond it goes around her face it goes down to her shoulders she turns the water on she checks the temperature.

I put Floyd up over my shoulder she pulls off his jumpsuit she pulls off his diaper I put Floyd on the seat in the shower she puts the straps on him.

"Okay, Harris," she says, "I got it from here. Thanks." She turns on the shower I leave I shut the door I go to the window there's a big field in the back part of the Ranch.

To the right of the big field there's bunkhouses and a dirt road the dirt road goes around in a circle the old ladies stay in the bunkhouses below us after that there's the girl camper and counselor bunkhouse after that there's the boy camper and counselor bunkhouse after that there's the ranch hand bunkhouse it's way in the back back where the circle road turns to the right Cosmic and Jolly stay there.

Coming back around this way outside the circle road there's the hayloft and storage barn and the mountain of rocks the mountain of rocks is behind the barn the corral and the stables are in the middle of the circle.

Rudy Dude's house is not on the circle road it's behind The Big House Cosmic says there's a trail behind Rudy Dude's house he says it leads to a theater in the mountains.

At the end of the big field way in the back back part of the ranch there's a campground the campground road starts at the circle road near the ranch hand bunkhouse and goes to the left next to the big field next to the bottom of the mountains there's brown and green mountains all around the ranch.

There's knocking and a voice I go to the door I open it there's no one there I close the door there's still knocking now there's singing I go to the bathroom door I put my ear on the door the knocking and singing are coming from there the singing is turning to screaming screaming it's Nurse Cannary screaming I open the door Nurse Cannary is bouncing up and down up and down on top of Floyd's lap her head is back and her eyes are closed and water is falling off of her hair into Floyd's face her hand is pulling her green bathing suit to the side and Floyd's pee pee going up up inside her she's going up up and down up up and down over and over my pee pee gets bigger I reach out to grab it my hand hits the doorknob Nurse Cannary opens her eyes she doesn't stop bouncing she looks at me she says, "Harris, I'm cleaning his pee pee. This is washing Floyd's pee pee," she keeps bouncing I close the door I go sit down on on my bed.

My pee pee is hard it won't go down it hurts I lay back I unzip my jumpsuit I take it out of my underwear I grab it I pull it it gets bigger and harder I pull it more and faster something starts happening something's happened it's happening something's going to come out of my pee pee Nurse Cannary cracks open the door she says, "Harris?" it comes out of my pee pee it goes into my face Nurse Cannary looks in she says, "Harris?" again then, "Oh, I'm sorry. Whenever you're ready, whenever you're ready, honey," she closes the door.

I clean up with the sheet I help Nurse Cannary get Floyd out of the shower I help him get dressed and back in his chair.

Nurse Cannary sits on my bed. "Come here for a second, Harris, okay?" I go over I sit down. "Sweetheart, there is nothing to be ashamed of, nothing at all, okay? Look at me honey. Nothing at all. It's all, all perfectly natural and normal, okay? Okay, honey?"

"Okay," I say.

She smiles I smile.

"Wait a minute. Harris. Did you just…You did." She gives me a hug. "That's great, Harris." She stands up she points to her watch. "Well all right, boys. Doc Holiday's in ten." She goes to the door. "He's going to be thrilled, Harris. But only if you want. It'll be your surprise." She leaves.

Floyd turns his Chair toward me. "I apologize, Oracle. It was not my intention that you should witness that. I meant no disrespect."

"Floyd. Floyd, would Nurse Cannary wash my pee pee too? Would, would she would wash my pee pee? How she was washing your pee pee, Floyd?"

He drives over to me he stops. "Oracle, I must confess, I'm confused. I assumed that, as Oracle, you would not be interested in such things, but obviously, that assumption was incorrect. And now I can see there is semen in your hair, above your right ear, forcing the further inference that...that's what took you so long coming to Martha Jane's assistance getting me out of the shower. You'll have to excuse me. I need a minute. He drives to the window.

Semen is the thick white fluid containing sperm that the male ejaculates I go to the bathroom I come back Floyd turns around.

"Oracle, I have a question or two for you, the answers to which might clear things up."

"Clear things up, yes, Floyd, clear things up."

"Okay. Oracle, what is an Oracle."

I say the songs that oracle is there are seven.

"Tell me the first one again, please," he says.

"Oracle is someone or something considered to be a source of knowledge, wisdom, or prophecy."

"Right. Now, what is someone."

"Someone is somebody."

"What is somebody."

"Somebody is some unspecified person."

"What is a person."

"A person is an individual human being."

"What is a human being."

"A human being is a member of the species to which men and women belong."

"What is a man."

"A man is an adult male human being."

"What is a male."

"A person or animal belonging to the sex that produces sperm."

"All right. Thank you, Oracle. I am sorry to ask so much of you at once. I don't want to abuse your charity. But Oracle. Sorry. One more thing."

WINTER PARK

"Yes, Floyd?"

"It would upset me if Martha Jane washed your pee pee."

39

Doc Holiday opens the door I go over to the window the window looks out over the front part of the Ranch.

"Well hello to you too, Mr. Birdsong," Doc Holiday says. "Good evening Mr. Floyd. How are you?"

"Very well, thank you. How are you?" Floyd says.

"Good, good. Yes, well, you two certainly seem in good spirits."

"Yes, we are in good spirits," Floyd says.

"Mr. Birdsong? Harris? Care to join me and Mr. Floyd this evening?"

I turn around. "Can, can I look out the window?"

"Well of c...hey, Harris, fantastic. It's great to hear your voice. But of course, my boy, of course, look all you want, but be a sport and do come over before too long, okay?"

"Okay."

Another dirt road goes in a circle around the front part of the Ranch there's a big building in the middle of the circle it says Dude Ranch Rodeo College on it that's what it says on the wall there's a dining hall and a kitchen and a auditorium and a library and classrooms the part with the auditorium and the library and the classrooms is two stories tall.

To the left outside the front circle road and to the right of the back circle road there are two small bunkhouses they're near the hayloft and storage barn the Mexicans stay there.

To the right outside of the front circle road there's the rodeo arena and the big parking lot me and Floyd consolidate rocks in the big parking lot.

Another road goes from the highway to the front circle road it goes in the gate and runs next to the rodeo arena the gate is antlers and rocks Rudy Dude says we can walk out it we can walk out it if we want there's nothing for a hundred miles.

Students are walking across the rodeo arena parking lot rodeo practice is over they they're going to the dining hall students practice rodeo in the afternoon they go to class in the morning.

"Yes, Wayne," Doc Holiday says, "strictly confidential. Unless you are planning on harming yourself or someone else, nothing you say gets beyond these walls. Now, Mr. Birdsong. Wayne was just about to tell me about a special talent of yours. Why don't you come on over."

"Okay," I say I go sit on the couch.

Doc Holiday wears glasses the glasses make his eyes look big there's a fish tank in the dining hall all the fish have big eyes Doc Holiday and the fish have big eyes Doc Holiday's hair is gone on the top he has hair on the sides he wears a white doctor's coat and a red tie and gray pants and white socks and brown sandals he always wears a white doctor's coat and a red tie and gray pants and white socks and brown sandals he always sits in a chair with me and Floyd the chair is on the rug he's tall and thin.

"But first," Doc Holiday says, "I'd love to know to what we owe the pleasure. Of your voice, Harris. Anything special happen this past week? Of course, there may be nothing, and we always knew you'd..."

"Floyd, Floyd's my friend."

Doc Holiday smiles and nods his head. "Yeah. A friend." He moves his head side to side. "Sometimes that's all it takes."

"He, The Oracle could always talk," Floyd says.

Doc Holiday turns to Floyd.

"But he only talked to me and only when prompted. Now he seems to be extemporizing."

Doc Holiday turns to me. "Harris, is that what you are, an oracle?"

"Oracle, Floyd, Floyd says I'm a oracle."

"And what is that, Harris? What is an oracle?"

"A oracle is seven things. The first one is to be a source of knowledge, wisdom, or prophecy."

"And is that what you are?"

"I, Floyd asks me things. I say what they are, I say what they are."

"Say what things are..." Doc Holiday writes on his pad he looks up. "Do you think you could show me what you mean, Harris?"

Floyd types. "I know. Open. Let's do open, from earlier today with Rudy Dude. Let's see if where we rake rocks is really a parking lot."

"Okay, Floyd."

"Okay then. Oracle, what is open."

I say the songs that open is Floyd stops me at one and ten and eleven and twenty-five he asks Doc Holiday to make a note of those I go to sixty-three I stop.

"Now, Oracle," Floyd says, "remind me, what, exactly, is a parking lot."

"Parking lot, an open area of ground in which people

can park their automobiles."

"And what is open essence number one again."

"Allowing people or things to pass through freely."

"And what is freely."

I say the songs that freely is there are seven.

"Just the first one again please, Oracle. Only that essence is relevant and applicable."

"Without restrictions, controls, or limits."

"What is a restriction."

"Something that limits or controls something else."

"What is a control."

"The limiting or restricting of something."

"And what is a limit."

I say the songs that limit is there are nine.

"Number four again, please."

"A feature or circumstance that restricts what can be done."

"Okay. Thank you, Oracle. The area where we rake rocks is not a parking lot in this case, under open essence number one. One reason is the big logs. They do not allow people or things to pass through freely. The logs that go around the whole area restrict where you can enter and exit and they restrict where you can place your foot and the logs inside the area restrict where you can drive and park and they also restrict where you can place your foot and even if there were no logs inside as soon as one car was parked in the area it would not be a parking lot anymore because the presence of one car restricts where you can drive or walk and you cannot pass through it freely. Okay. What is the next one, the next open essence, Doc."

"Ten."

"Having no boundaries or enclosures," I say.

"The logs are boundaries, obviously, so the area where we rake rocks is not a parking lot in this case either. Next one please, Doc."

"Eleven."

"Let's come back to eleven. Next one please, Doc."

"Twenty-five."

"Free from blockage and therefore allowing unobstructed passage," I say.

"It's the same problem again with the logs. They obstruct passage. Okay, number eleven. Is that the last one."

"Yes, Wayne. That's it," Doc Holiday says.

"Go ahead, Oracle."

"Okay. Having no cover or roof."

"Yes, this one is trickier. The area we where we rake rocks has no cover or roof, so in this case, under open essence number eleven, it is a parking lot. It is an area of ground with no cover or roof in which people can park their automobiles however this means the large covered area next to the auditorium and the dining hall where people can park their automobiles is not a parking lot and it cannot be a parking lot under any of the other essences of open either because the area also has restrictions on where you can drive or walk it has even more restrictions the sign that says 'Rodeo College Parking Lot' is incorrect and must be changed."

Doc Holiday sits forward in his chair. "Wow, fellows. I am impressed. You two have really come along, really made progress. What a difference a week can make." He sits back. "Where to begin. Well, okay, first of all, congratulations to both of you on the improvement of your communication and interpersonal skills. Tremendous improvement. Harris, you're speaking, to me now anyway, *and* you're a sage.

Wayne, the intensity and precision of your analytical thought are truly engaging. You're like a microscope. Rather vast improvement in your dexterity on those keyboards as well...though I should say, I think you manage to miss some punctuation, the comma and period bars specifically, when you really get cooking. That's something you might work on. But yes, yes, fantastic." Doc Holiday writes on his pad he looks up. "Now, let me ask you two a few questions. First, the standard. Have you noticed any changes in your memories? No? First memories for both of you are still waking up in your beds here?"

Floyd says, "Yes." I nod my head.

Doc Holiday looks down he writes on his pad he says to his pad, "Continued dehydration- and stroke-induced post-traumatic retrograde amnesia and identity loss, Mr. Floyd. Continued traumatic-epileptic retrograde amnesia and identity loss, Mr. Birdsong." He looks up. "Okay then," he says. "Harris. Where, oh where in the world does *all that* information come from?"

"It's inside my head, it's inside my head."

Doc Holiday drinks from his cup. "Mm, yes, of course." He puts the cup down on the desk. "But it has to have a source. What is the *source* of all that information in your head, Harris?"

"Source, source is the place where something begins, the thing from which something is derived, the person or group that created or initiated something."

"That's exactly right, Harris. Now do you know the source of all the information in your head?"

"It's inside, inside my head."

"All right, well, the reason I ask is that, what you're calling essences, Floyd, sound an awful lot like definition entries for words in a dictionary. Harris, have you…There's no way, I know, but…Do you know if you have somehow memorized or internalized a dictionary?"

"No, no, I don't know."

"Do you know what a dictionary is?"

"Yes, yes, it's six things. It's a reference book that contains words listed in alphabetical order and gives explanations of their meanings, it's…"

"Okay, Harris, that's right, that's good." Doc Holiday writes on his pad. "Thank you." He looks up. "But now, Harris, do you always understand this information, the information that comes to you?"

"No, no…no. I hear it, I always hear it."

"Okay." Doc Holiday writes on his pad he looks up. "Floyd. You use the word 'essence' here in connection with the information Harris provides. What does that mean? What do you mean by essence here?"

Floyd types. "The sound essence is only a word. All words do is help us identify things. One word can identify various things, and everything is a thing, from physical object to metaphysical object, or concept. What The Oracle gives us are essential descriptions, what I call the essences for short, of things in the world, not the definitions of the word, which is the sign that merely points to those things. I grant you, essences of things resemble definitions of words and that's exactly what I would think they were too were it not for the fact that as you suggested earlier it is impossible absolutely impossible for anyone to memorize a dictionary the best only explanation therefore is that the Oracle is not a dictionary but an unmediated reader of the essences of things that he has direct access to the a priori to the metaphysical model or blueprint of the universe that he reads conceptual reality directly that he reads directly the way things are and the limits of the way things can be."

Doc Holiday puts his pen in his mouth he is quiet he takes the pen out of his mouth. "But Wayne, Harris uses language to communicate, and language can't get at the essences of things because language is, by its very nature, media, is a mediation, isn't that right?"

"No, not if that language has no source or if its source is truly original and self-generating. If its source is truly original and self-generating, that language is the logos of the cosmos, it's the language of God, it's the word of God."

"I see." Doc Holiday writes on his pad he looks up. "Well, what does that make you, then, Wayne? The priest of the Oracle?"

"Yes. I interpret the information given by the Oracle. I determine the meaning of the various essences and, in ambiguous situations, I determine which essence is relevant and applicable given a particular context."

"Right...but then you'll have to admit that at least *you* are a medium, right? You mediate or interpret the language of the Oracle?"

"Yes. There is nothing I can do about that, except try to take the word of the Oracle as literally as possible when applying it to situations and contexts in the practical world. I treat everything he says, in his capacity as Oracle, as a true premise, and it's my job to determine what those premises entail."

Doc Holiday writes on his pad he looks up. "Harris, what is it like...in what way...how exactly do you receive this information?"

"Different songs, it's different little songs," I say.

"Different little songs." Doc writes on his pad he looks

up. "You mean, each def...each essence you hear, each essence is a different little song?"

"Yes, yes."

"The music of the universe," Floyd says.

"Mm, may be," Doc says. "Harris, are you hearing songs all the time? Is the information coming in to you in songs all the time, like right now?"

"No, no, right now I hear the outside, I hear the outside all the time. If I want to I can hear the notes and songs."

"Right, right, sorry. You initiate. That's good. It's hard to imagine one could function otherwise, isn't it?" Doc Holiday laughs. "So how long, do you know how long you've had this ability?"

"No, no, I don't know."

Doc Holiday writes on his pad he looks up. "Mr. Floyd, when did you discover that Mr. Birdsong has this ability? What were the circumstances?"

"It was a couple of weeks ago. It's just now I am confident enough to talk about it, with you. I suspected him of being the Oracle because he occasionally showed, when I prompted him, precise knowledge about certain things, but I became certain the time we were consolidating rocks and I was wondering what the essence of an automobile is. I remember, he said, an automobile is a road vehicle designed to carry a small number of passengers, and I became concerned that either that wasn't right or vehicles designed to carry drivers are not really automobiles and that we are misusing the term automobile however through a concatenation of responses to an extensive series of carefully considered queries he it was demonstrated that the human subject has imperfections that duality is an imperfection that the mind/body duality is a human imperfection that mind is to driver as passenger is to body that a human subject can be both driver and passenger at the same time and that automobiles therefore are in fact road vehicles designed to carry a small number of passengers and all my concerns were dispelled. Sorry. It was by virtue of the sheer volume of his knowledge and the beauty of the proof that I became convinced he is the Oracle, that his essential descriptions of things are always correct, and that any misuse of concomitant terms lies with people. And it was by virtue of the very particular nature of our dialogical inquiry that I became convinced that he is my Oracle. You see, one has to know how to ask the right questions and follow the right threads to get reliable, responsible results. The Oracle and I, we are a team now."

"Why do you think the Oracle makes it so hard on you then, Wayne? Why doesn't he give you, as the essence of automobile, a road vehicle designed to carry a small number of passengers *and a driver*? You see - not to be contentious, Wayne - but to me, it's more likely just a bad definition of automobile."

"No. Again, not when we know Harris could not have memorized a dictionary. It is not for us to question why the metaphysical expresses itself through the Oracle the way that it does. His is the more original way, and it is my job to track a way back through the accumulated overgrowth, to decipher his true meanings. Sometimes he speaks in mysterious ways."

Doc Holiday writes on his pad. "All right, well, listen..." He looks up. "This is a lot for me to take in. So, let me just ask you both, besides the ones we've been discussing, have there been any other major changes or breakthroughs in your lives over the past week, since we last met? Or anything else you'd like to share with me? Mr. Birdsong? You have something?"

"Yes, yes, I have something."

"All right, go ahead."

"I made semen come out of my pee pee today."

"Ah. Right. That is big, no pun intended." Doc Holiday laughs. "Well, tell me, then, Harris, how was that?"

"Good. Messy. That semen got in my face, it got in my hair."

Doc Holiday writes on his pad he looks up. "I bet. But so what brought this on?"

"I, I saw Nurse Cannary washing Floyd's pee pee in the shower. My pee pee got big, it got hard, it wouldn't go down, it wouldn't go down. It hurt. I got in the bed. I took my pee pee out. I held it and pulled it. I pulled it, that's when the semen came out, it came out of my pee pee."

Doc Holiday writes on his pad. "I see. Well, Harris..." He looks up. "Floyd's pee pee has got to get washed somehow...Were you spying on them, Harris?"

"Yes, yes, I was spying on them, I heard banging. Nurse Cannary was screaming, I opened the door. I saw, saw Nurse Cannary, she, she was washing Floyd's pee pee in the shower."

"What happ..." Doc Holiday says Floyd types. "Why was Nurse Cannary screa'..."

"She slipped and bumped her head on the metal rail but she was fine," Floyd says. "It was more like a little yelp, not a scream."

"Ah. I see," Doc Holiday says he writes on his pad.

"Yes," Floyd says, "and Doc, this is also how I found out the Oracle is a human being."

Doc Holiday looks up. "What? Whoa. Why? Because he

masturbates?"

Masturbates masturbate is to give oneself or somebody else sexual pleasure by stroking the genitals.

"Yes. When I saw semen in his hair, I knew he had masturbated, and he wouldn't have if he weren't human."

"Monkeys masturbate, Wayne."

"Yes, but he does not look like a monkey."

"Yeah, all right, well..." Doc Holiday writes on his pad he looks up. "Did this surprise you, Wayne? Did it surprise you to discover that Harris is human?"

"Yes. He had never given me any reason to believe he was anything but some sort of objective entity housed in a human body, like an android. Well, earlier today, he did taunt me, and then he gave me some advice in the elevator. I thought that was strange, different. But before that, all he ever did was respond to my inquiries. He never once voiced or otherwise displayed his own thoughts or opinions or desires."

"So you were confused?"

"Yes, because I thought that an oracle could only be an objective entity, and that if he's not an objective entity then he's not an oracle, but then I had witnessed with my own eyes and ears his seemingly infinite ability to access the very essences of things and I knew he had to be an oracle because there was no other explanation. So this afternoon I asked the Oracle himself to enlighten me, and he did. He showed me that an oracle can be someone as well as something, that a personal entity can contain objective information as well as an impersonal one, and that oracles can masturbate without compromising the transmission of objective information."

Doc Holiday writes on his pad he stops he looks at his

watch he puts his pad and pen on his desk. "All right, fellows." He smiles. "We're out of time. But before I forget..." He digs in his coat pocket he takes something out it's a little silver phone Rudy Dude has one Rudy Dude uses one. "Here, Harris." He holds it out for me. "Nurse Cannary and I want you to carry this cell phone with you, in case of emergency. We should have gotten you one a long time ago, but..."

I stand up I take it I sit back down.

"All you have to do is flip it open and press one and it'll dial Nurse Cannary directly. There's no use trying to call other numbers on it. It's been fixed so the only number you can dial is Nurse Cannary and the only number you can receive is Nurse Cannary. It's like a walkie-talkie. Go ahead. Flip it open and press one."

I open it I press one I hold the phone up to my ear.

"No, sorry, here Harris. Also press the speaker button." Doc Holiday gets up he shows me. "See. Press this button, this little symbol, so we can all hear." There's ringing.

"Hello Harris," Nurse Cannary says.

"Hi Martha Jane. It's Doc Holiday and Mr. Birdsong and Mr. Floyd."

"Hi," she says.

"Well, say 'hi' fellows...Okay, we're just testing the cell phone to see if it works. It does," Doc Holiday laughs Nurse Cannary laughs. "We're wrapping things up in here. It's about your dinner time too, isn't it fellows?"

"It's chicken strips today, Doc," Nurse Cannary says. "Chicken strips and green beans. I'll bring it over to your room shortly, Harris. Got you covered too, Wayne. Bye."

"Bye," Doc Holiday says. "Okay Harris, now snap it shut."

40

We eat dinner in the room I eat dinner Nurse Cannary pulls up Floyd's shirt there's a tube there's a tube in his stomach she holds up the tube she takes off the top there's a bag on a pole it has yellow juice in it it has a tube too Nurse Cannary puts the tubes together the yellow juice goes down the tube it goes into Floyd's stomach that's Floyd's dinner that's how Floyd has dinner Nurse Cannary sits down she opens a book she reads a story the story's about a man the man's name is Don and his friend his friend's name is Sancho they ride horses they ride horses around they get in fights Floyd falls asleep Nurse Cannary gets up and fixes Floyd's chair she makes it flat.

"Sorry Wayne," she says. "Just trying to make sure you're comfortable."

"That's okay. Thank you."

"I'll just get your blanket."

Nurse Cannary gets a blanket from the closet and puts it on him she gives him a kiss kiss. "Good night, Wayne." She goes to the door she switches off the light. "Good night, Harris."

"Good night, good night," I say she leaves.

There's a silver light across Floyd's face it's coming in the curtains I get up it's the moon the moon is full the moon is silver the silver light is from the moon everything outside

WINTER PARK

is silver and black I close the curtains I get back in bed.

41

Me and Floyd are in the rodeo arena parking lot we're consolidating rocks Chip Geener says, "Excuse me everyone, can I have your attention, please?" Chip Geener's on the speakers the speakers are outside all over the ranch they're on poles he says for everyone everyone to go to the auditorium now go to the auditorium for a big surprise.

Me and Floyd go to the auditorium we go in the auditorium there's no one there it's dark it's quiet we sit I sit in the back back Floyd stays in the aisle he sits in his chair in the aisle next to me more people come in Cosmic and Jolly come in Laura Tate and Sarah Castleberry come in Rachel Hill and Jackie Sherwood come in David Hill comes in students come in Mexicans come in Doc Holiday and Nurse Cannary come in Rudy Dude comes in and old ladies old ladies come in no more no more people come in everybody's in the auditorium everybody's talking everybody's talking there's a big surprise Floyd doesn't know Floyd doesn't know what the big surprise is nobody knows what the big surprise is the giant screen turns blue.

"Okay. Test. Okay, everyone, can I have your attention, please?" It's Chip Geener he's on the speakers people turn around I turn around Chip Geener's behind us he's in the little glass room he's in the back back. "Please stop talking. Everyone, please. Please stop talking. We are about to begin." Everyone keeps talking talking.

Sounds sounds come on the speakers everyone stops talking everyone looks at the screen the screen is blue the screen is blue and there are sounds sounds of someone doing something someone's doing something somewhere breathing moving things around the screen is blue a door creaks a woman says, "Oh Shit!" a chair scrapes across the floor there are footsteps footsteps. "What in the world..." the woman says the door creaks again. "No, no. Come here, Preston." The woman's voice gets quieter quieter maybe in another room she may be in another room. "Not now, okay. Occupado. Now come on. Vamanos. En tu caurto, ahorita." Another door creaks it's quieter the footsteps get quieter quieter quieter the footsteps are gone in front of the auditorium a lady screams she screams and cries it's a Mexican lady she's screaming and crying she won't stop she won't stop she won't stop screaming and crying two men stand up they go get her the two men are Mexicans they take her out out of her seat and down the aisle and out of the doors everyone's looking everyone's talking the footsteps come back on the speakers the footsteps everybody gets quiet a quiet door creaks on the speakers it shuts the footsteps get louder another door creaks it shuts the footsteps get louder the chair scrapes across the floor the woman says, "God almighty Jesus..." The chair scrapes again papers maybe things get moved there's a click she breathes in she breathes out. "Okay," she says a woman comes onto the screen she's big her head and face and shoulders and chest are big her arms are big she's got straight yellow hair it comes down to her shoulders she's wearing a yellow sweater she has on thick glasses there are papers in front of her there's a cigarette in a ashtray it's burning burning it's smoking there's a moose moosehead on the wall. "Chip. Chip," she says, "is this thing on? Are we running?"

Chip runs down the aisle he runs up onto the stage he stands in the light. "Yes, Warden Dude. We can see you and hear you loud and clear. Can you see and hear us?"

"Yeah. But now what in the..."

"Warden Dude? Warden Dude? Warden Dude, I'm guessing what you're concerned about is your own image in your PIP? Is that your concern? Warden, the PIP is a reference, a monitor, so you can see what we see, so you can make sure we can see you. Warden?"

"Yeah, no, I know what a..." Warden Dude is looking for something. "Jesus." She shakes her head she picks up some papers. "Ah." She puts down the papers in front of her. "All right," she says she looks up. "Ready?"

"Yes ma'am. We're rolling. Ready when you are." Chip goes to the side of the stage he turns off the light.

"All right, well, surpri'..." Warden Dude starts coughing she coughs she leans over she coughs a long time she sits up she inhales she coughs again hard. "Jesus H. Christ...anyway...surprise. It's me. I'm the surprise."

Chip Geener starts clapping. "Woo hoo!" He looks out at us he claps. "Woo hoo! Come on! Warden Dude, everybody, yeah!" He claps.

"All right, just get outta here," Warden Dude says she looks down at Chip Geener Chip Geener stops clapping he turns around he looks up at Warden Dude he points to himself.

"Yeah you, Pippy, but before you go, do me a favor. Look at that piece of paper I sent you. That's right, it's on your little clipboard. Now read item number two, *to yourself*. I'll tell everybody what it says. It says, 'No clapping: please inform everyone to hold all noise, including clapping, until the Warden has signed off the transmission'. You are an excitable toad. Now get outta here." Chip Geener walks across the stage he goes down down the steps he goes into the aisle. "That's it, go on. Shew." Warden Dude flips her hand at him Chip Geener bursts into tears he runs out of the auditorium someone stands up in the front row he goes toward the aisle Warden Dude watches he steps into the aisle it's David Hill.

"Well, I reckon somebody's got to go out and hold his hand," Warden Dude says she waits David Hill goes out the doors. "All right. Now. I, I am Warden Judy Dude, and today I am going to tell y'all a little story. It's a story about telling stories. It's called 'The Mayor of Littleton'. So sit tight and listen up and don't nobody move until I'm done.

"Once upon a time there was a lady named Ms. Delia who was the mayor of a very small town called Littleton. She lived all alone in a big house, but at least once every day she would leave her house to go out and visit with the townspeople, and she never, ever missed the big celebration that was held every spring in the town square. She always dressed up like a cowgirl. All the townspeople loved Ms. Delia.

"Then one spring she missed the big celebration that was held in the town square. She did not dress up like a cowgirl. And the following week, she stopped leaving her house and going out to talk to the townspeople. The townspeople thought this was very strange.

"When Ms. Delia did not come out a second week, the townspeople called her on the phone and asked her to come out and visit with them, like before, but she politely declined. Then Ms. Delia asked them if they would please leave some food and supplies for her in her garage, which she would leave open. The townspeople did what Ms. Delia asked, and Ms. Delia closed her garage.

"When Ms. Delia did not come out a third week, Ms. Delia's cousin, Tim, called a town meeting. 'I warned you about Ms. Delia a long time ago,' he said, 'but you all wouldn't listen. You should have voted me mayor. She is not fit for the job!' But the townspeople did not agree. They *loved* Ms. Delia. Still, they were very concerned about her and their town, so they agreed with Tim that they should at least keep a close eye on Ms. Delia's house.

"Over the fourth week, the townspeople watched Ms. Delia's house. Through the windows they could see her moving from room to room, and they could see when she turned the lights on and off at night.

"At the end of the fourth week, Ms. Delia called the townspeople on the phone and asked them to deliver *ten times* the amount of food and supplies to her garage as last time. They agreed but were beginning to wonder if Tim was right about Ms. Delia. The townspeople became even *more* frightened when, over the fifth week, because the lights were always off, they could no longer see Ms. Delia moving from room to room in her house.

"The townspeople started to panic. They called Ms. Delia on the phone, but there was no answer. They knocked on her door, but there was no answer. Finally, at the end of the fifth week, they came to Tim in desperation, and another town meeting was called.

"At the meeting, each of the townspeople was given a chance to say what he or she thought was wrong with Ms. Delia. Some said she was *ill*; some said she had gone *crazy*;

some said she was *depressed*; others said she had somehow slipped out and gone on holiday; and one said she was simply taking a much deserved break. Then they fell to arguing.

"'Order!' Tim cried. 'We must have order!' The townspeople went quiet. 'Now,' Tim said. 'We must get to the bottom of this. The wellbeing of Littleton is at stake! For, my friends, however much it pains us, we must accept the possibility that, at this point, Ms. Delia could even be *dead*.' The townspeople gasped. 'And I'm sorry, but what good, I ask you, is a dead mayor? We must *demand* a satisfactory explanation from Ms. Delia herself. In the event that one is not forthcoming, I will be forced to take over the mayorship of Littleton.' Many of the townspeople cried, but they all agreed with Tim, and a plan was hatched to write a note to Ms. Delia demanding that she explain herself, otherwise Tim would be named mayor.

"The next night, Tim and his assistant went to Ms. Delia's house, tied the note to a rock, and threw it through her living room window. Several days passed, but much to the townspeople's chagrin, there was no reply from Ms. Delia.

"On the day Tim was to become mayor of Littleton, the townspeople decided to try one last time to get Ms. Delia to come out of her house and explain herself. They made signs that said, 'Delia Come Out,' and 'Delia Please,' and carried them over to her house in the morning and began to chant, 'Come out, come out, wherever you are!' But the whole day passed without a sign from Ms. Delia.

"As the sun set and the townspeople's shadows grew long, Tim drove up in his big blue car. He got out and said, 'Okay folks, let's wrap it up. I have the new mayorship papers right here.' He held them up in the air. 'So if everyone will just take a minute to come over and sign, we can start being a real town again.'

"But just as everyone was about to give up on Ms. Delia and sign the papers, they heard something rip through the air. It was an arrow, shot from inside Ms. Delia's house, out the hole in the window made by the rock. A little boy staggered and fell. The townspeople gathered around him and screamed and cried, but there was nothing they could do. The arrow had pierced the little boy's heart. Within minutes he was dead.

"A young girl, his sister, came up close to the body and pointed at the arrow. 'What? What is it? What do you see?' the townspeople said. A message had been carved in the arrow's shaft. She read it out loud: 'For reasons all my own.'"

The Warden smiles she leans forward she holds up a finger. "All right, everybody. You may clap..." Her finger goes down. "Now," she says the screen turns blue.

42

"Hey man. Hey, did you guys hear?" Jolly says. "We got the rest of the day off."

"Seriously," Floyd says.

"Yeah, man. It's awesome." Jolly's short and skinny he talks real fast. "Rudy came up to me after the Warden's thing in there and told me. He said he has to go deal with the Mexicans or something. Let's go do archery."

"I could get stoked for that," Cosmic says. "Yeah, sure, dude. Let's go."

"You have on a different, a different hat, Cosmic," I say.

"Oh, yeah, dude, I do. Thanks for noticing." Cosmic's tall and skinny and white he talks real slow. "I've been like, switching this one out for the sombrero sometimes because the sombrero like, gives me a headache. I mean, don't get me wrong, bro. I'd way rather wear the sombrero. That's a dude hat. This here's a floppy ladies' sun hat, I know, but it fits better. It's like, looser, and obviously I like, have to wear a hat, so...Hey, wait a minute, dude. Did you just say something?" He turns to Jolly. "Did Birdsong just say something?"

"Yeah, man, I think he did. I think he just said something. I don't think I've heard him say a word since we've been here."

"Cosmic, wow. Well, good to hear it, Birdsong."

I get my hat it's under Floyd's chair it's in the basket under Floyd's chair I leave Floyd's beret in the basket I take out the umbrella I put it on Floyd's chair it's sunny it's hot.

"All right, dudes," Cosmic says. "Let's go shoot some arrows."

We head to the big field.

"So that was a wicked bad story the warden told, right?" Jolly says.

"I don't know, bro," Cosmic says. "I thought it was pretty dark. It was like...yeah, dark."

"It was an allegory," Floyd says.

"What's an allegory?" Cosmic says.

"I know," I say Floyd types, "allegory is..." Floyd says, "is a story whose characters represent real people and whose message is really intended for them."

"What?" Jolly says.

"The townspeople are really all the people at Dude Ranch; Ms. Delia is really Warden Dude; Tim is really Rudy Dude; and the message is really from Warden Dude to Rudy Dude and the people at Dude Ranch. The message is: 'Whatever I do is my own business so stop being so nosy and leave me alone; if you don't, people are going to get hurt, people are going to die."

"Jesus Christ," Cosmic says.

"Yeah, man. That's fucked, that's fucked up," Jolly says.

"But like wait a minute." Cosmic says. "What about the little boy, Floyd? Who is he like, *really*, at the Ranch?"

"I don't know. He's innocent, he's a victim, but who he is really, at the Ranch, I don't know."

We walk everybody's quiet we come to a shed it's in the big field Jolly opens the shed the shed's got bows and arrows and rakes and shovels in it Jolly takes out bows and arrows.

"You'll shoot one too, won't you, Floyd?" Jolly says. "You can use your hands and fingers, right?"

"Yes, I'll shoot one," Floyd says. "I can shoot it."

"Cool. Here you go, Birdsong." Jolly gives me a bow and arrows. "Cosmic." He gives Cosmic a bow and arrows.

"What's that?" I ask I point to a wooden structure in the corner of the field in the back corner of the field it's a wooden box in the air on stilts with a ladder under it the ladder goes straight up into the box.

"What? That thing?" Jolly says. "Where the road ends? That's the jail. Well, it's really a deer blind, or a hunting blind, but they call it the jail." A jail is a secure place for keeping people awaiting legal judgment. "Story is they started calling it the jail at the same time they started bringing on troubled people and delinquents, like us, as ranch hands. You know, just in case one of us got out of hand. I've never heard of anybody being put in there yet, though. Why do you ask, Birdsong? You interested in trying it out?

"No, no."

Jolly laughs. "All right then, we're ready to go." He closes the shed. "Come on over here." We follow him.

"Okay, see this rope right here, stretched on the ground?" Jolly points with his toe. "That's the line, the shooting line. You can put your toe, or your wheel, on it, but not past it. Don't go past it. That's illegal. And that's it. Now just line up across from one of those targets." He points with his finger there's ten round targets they have red and blue and black circles on them there's hay bales behind them back back behind them. "And fire away, like this, watch this, I'll show you how it's done." Jolly takes his hat off he throws it on the ground he drops a lot of arrows on the ground he keeps one arrow in his hand he's put it up into the bow he shoots it it makes a sound it stops in the target.

"See, bulls-eye," Jolly says.

"Wow," Cosmic says. "You still got it, dude."

Jolly smiles Cosmic steps up to the rope he can't get the arrow to stay on the string to stay on the string in the bow he drops the arrow he picks it up he drops the arrow he picks it up.

"Take off your hat," Jolly says.

Cosmic takes off his hat he drops the arrow he picks it up he puts it on the string in the bow he pulls the string he shoots it he shoots the arrow it goes onto the ground in front of him he puts down the bow he goes over the rope line he picks up the arrow he comes back he picks up the bow he puts the arrow on the string in the bow he pulls the string he shoots it he shoots the arrow nobody sees it nobody sees where the arrow went it's gone.

I stand up at the line I try to get the arrow on the string it's hard it's hard to get the arrow on the string in the bow I get it I shoot it I shoot all the arrows all the arrows go in the dirt in the grass one goes into the hay.

"Not bad, Birdsong, not bad," Jolly says. "All right, now let's see if we can get Floyd going."

Floyd drives up to the line Jolly brings him a bow and arrow. "You're right-handed, right?"

"Yes."

"Cool." Jolly kneels beside Floyd he puts the bow and arrow on the ground he puts his hand on Floyd's right keyboard. "Can I move this?"

"Yes, I got it." Floyd presses something under the keyboard the keyboard moves over to the left.

Jolly picks up the bow he picks it up in his right hand he

grabs the handle he holds it up in front of Floyd.

With his left hand Jolly takes Floyd's fingers he puts Floyd's fingers onto the string. "Hold it tight." He reaches down he picks up the arrow he picks it up he lays the front of the arrow onto the bow he puts the back back of the arrow into Floyd's fingers he puts it into Floyd's fingers and onto the string. "Tight on the string, light on the arrow. Yeah, right. And balanced on the bow. Good." Jolly moves his left hand he moves it from Floyd's fingers to Floyd's arm he holds down Floyd's arm.

"Okay, let's do it," Jolly says he pushes the bow he pushes it he extends his arm in front of Floyd away from Floyd he pushes it he pushes it the bow is bent the string is tight. "All right, Floyd. Whenever you're ready." Floyd lets go the arrow shoots it hits the target it hits the red ring.

"Dude," Cosmic says a telephone rings.

Jolly stands up. "What the hell was that?"

"Phone, phone," I say, "It's the phone, for emergency. Doc Holiday gave me a phone for emergency."

"Well, you better answer it," Jolly says.

I take it out of my pocket it says, 'Nurse Cannary calling...' I open it. "Hello, hello."

"Hi Harris," she says it's Nurse Cannary.

"Hello, hi."

"What are y'all doing?"

"Shooting, shooting archery with Cosmic and Jolly"

"Oh, archery, that sounds fun. Is Wayne available? Or is he too busy shooting?"

"Yes. He's, Floyd's shooting."

"Harris."

"Yes."

"Put Wayne on. And don't forget to put it on speaker

please, honey, okay. I need to speak with him right away, thank you. I'll hold."

I press the speaker button I put the phone in Floyd's lap the keyboard moves under his hand Floyd drives away he drives into the field Nurse Cannary says, "Wayne, honey, don't drive while I'm talking to you, please." Floyd stops. "That's better. So listen, honey, I need you to come on back to the infirmary, right now. We need to run some tests, check your fluid levels, get you cleaned up, all right? I know you got the afternoon off, but go ahead and wrap up what you're doing, shooting arrows and whatever it is, and come on back to the room. You hear me? Wayne?"

"Yes, but..."

"No, Wayne. No buts. I have urgent medical procedures I am required to conduct on you, back here, at the infirmary, on the double, mister. Your health is at stake, Wayne, so get a move on."

"All right." Floyd drives back over to me I take the phone I snap it shut.

"Damn, man," Jolly says.

"Yeah, dude, that was like, totally harsh," Cosmic says. "She harshed on your buzz, bad, bro."

"I better go. Thanks, Jolly." Floyd drives away across the big field.

43

It's morning me and Floyd are going to the storage barn we're going to the storage barn to get the snowplow and the rake we're going to consolidate rocks we always do that David Hill David Hill comes on the speakers he says, "Attention everyone. Attention everyone at Dude Ranch. This is instructor David Hill. Good morning. I have an important announcement to make.

"Chip Geener, instructor, dude-brother, friend, and highly valued member of the Dude Ranch family, has gone missing. He disappeared yesterday afternoon, after the Warden's gathering in the auditorium. I was the last one to see him." David Hill starts crying.

"Excuse me. He said he just needed to take a walk, to clear his head. He said the meeting in the auditorium had been really stressful for him. I told him I was happy to go, to go with him, that I *wanted* to go with him, but he said, no, he just wanted to be alone for a while.

"I last saw him..." David Hill cries he cries again. "I last saw him walking toward the back part of the Ranch, in the direction of the big hayloft and storage barn. I assume he was heading into the mountains on the Limpia Creek Trail. Chip and I hike that trail a lot. But I don't know. He could've been heading over to the campground and the trails back there. I don't know.

"Okay." David Hill sniffles. "Now, if anyone has any information about where Chip is, or might have gone, please come to the registration desk *immediately*. And everyone please, *please* keep an eye and an ear out for him. But also, *please* do not attempt any heroic rescue missions on your own. There are mountain lions, and bears, and javelinas out there..." David Hill starts crying he cries a lot he stops. "An official, an official rescue search will be initiated when and if necessary. We can't have any of us getting hurt.

"Now, I'm...Roberta and I are going to sing a little song for Chip in hopes that he will hear it." David plays his guitar he sings:

"Chip, Chip Jesus will find you / Chip, Chip, he's right behind you / Shining his light through the trees. He's got the light and he's fighting behind you / Bearing the load of your plight. Chip, Chip, Chip / Braving the wilderness alone. Chip, Chip, Chip / Jesus will carry you home.

"Chip, Chip Geener. If you can hear me, please, *please* come back, come back to the ranch. Come back to the ranch, right now. Chip...Okay. Thank you all for your attention."

"What, what happened to Chip Geener?" I say I grab the snowplow.

"I don't know, Harris," Floyd says. "While I am not fond of Geener, I hate to imagine that something horrible and painful has happened to him, like falling off a cliff, or being eaten by javelinas. That's empathy."

"Empathy is the abili..."

"Harris, Oracle, would you mind not volunteering essences, or saying what things are, without a formal prompt from me, or without my first saying, Oracle, what is so-and-so. That's standard oracle protocol. I have to consult you first, okay."

"Okay, Floyd."

"Okay, so Oracle, what is empathy, please."

"Empathy is the ability to identify with and understand another person's feelings or difficulties."

"Yes. Even though I am not fond of Geener, I can still empathize with him, in his current plight, if he is in one. This amounts to putting myself in his shoes. Still, it's puzzling though because if I put myself in his shoes he's not in his shoes anymore and it's my pain not his I'm imagining so technically empathy is still selfish. Anyway, you realize, we don't really know what has happened to Geener yet, Harris. He might be fine. He might have just gone home."

I attach the snowplow to Floyd's chair I grab my rake.

"Harris, let's take that paint over there and that brush too."

"Okay." I get the paint and brush I put them in Floyd's lap. "What are we going to paint, Floyd?"

"You'll see."

Floyd drives out of the barn I follow him he stops at the Rodeo College Parking Lot sign.

"All right," he says. "What should we change it to, Rodeo College Parking, or Rodeo College Lot. Oracle, please, what is a lot?"

I say the songs that lot is there are ten.

"Number five again, please, Oracle."

"A small area of land that has fixed boundaries."

"And what is land?"

I say the songs that land is there are seventeen.

"Numbers one, two, four, and six again, please."

"One is the solid part of the earth's surface not covered by a body of water. Two is a part of the earth's surface of a particular kind or that is used for a particular purpose. Four is an area of ground that somebody owns. Six is an area, domain, or realm that is notable for something."

"Six seems the most general. Let's start with number six. The area under scrutiny must be notable for something. What else could that be but parking. There is nothing else to say about it. So, in order for this area to be both land and lot, the parking here must be notable, or parking in general must be notable. So, what is notable, please, Oracle?"

I say the songs that notable is there are three.

"Okay, the first two are relevant and applicable. Say number two again, please, Oracle."

"Two is interesting, significant, and worth calling attention to."

"Okay, the parking here, or parking in general has to be all three, interesting, significant, and worth calling attention to, and it is none of those things. So what's number one again, please, Oracle?"

"One is significant or great enough to deserve attention or to be recorded."

"Interesting. To be notable, parking must be one of four things: significant enough to deserve attention, significant enough to be recorded, great enough to deserve attention, or great enough to be recorded, and since there is nothing significant or great at all about the parking here, or parking in general..."

"What, what's wrong, Floyd?"

"This is taking too long. Why don't we tr...Oracle, what is parking."

Number one sings I say number one number two sings I say number two number three...

"Yes, that's exactly it." Floyd says. "Spaces in which a vehicle may be parked. You can stop there please, Oracle.

Thank you very much. Now, Harris, would you please paint over the word 'lot' on the sign so it reads simply, Rodeo College Parking."

"Floyd. Do you think we're going to get into trouble with Rudy Dude, Floyd? I, I don't want to get in trouble with Rudy Dude, Floyd."

"We're not going to get into trouble, Harris. Don't be a scaredy-cat. The sign is incorrect. We are correcting it. We're doing the Ranch a favor. We should charge them a fee. Okay, Harris, if you're that worried about it. Listen: Oracle, what is incorrect."

"One is wrong, false, or inaccurate. Two is not appropriate, suitable, or proper."

"Exactly. You see, Harris. We are merely righting a wrong; making something that was false, true; making something improper, proper."

"Okay, Floyd. If you say so, Floyd."

I start painting the sign.

"It's not always but almost always best to follow the more parsimonious analysis, and in this case we had nothing to lose and everything to gain by doing so."

I paint.

"Harris," Floyd says. "I know you're busy and I don't want to bother the Oracle with it right now, but I've been thinking about doing a more formal, philosophical investigation into the essential formation and formulation of parking lots. Would you and the Oracle mind sitting down and helping me with that sometime, soon, maybe at night, before going to bed, instead of story-time."

"Okay, Floyd," I say. "I, we don't mind."

"Thanks. That would be wonderful."

"All right, all done." I step back from the sign.

"Let's see. Oh, yes. Harris, that looks great. It's perfect. Now let's get out of here."

Floyd drives to the rodeo arena parking lot I take the paint and brush I take my rake I run I put the paint and brush back back in the storage barn I run out of the storage barn I run past the sign the sign we painted Rudy Dude's pickup truck is in the rodeo arena parking lot I run I get closer Rudy Dude is sitting in his pickup truck he's talking to Floyd.

"Where you been?" Rudy Dude says.

"I forgot my rake, I forgot my rake," I say I breathe in and out.

"Well how in the hell could you..." Rudy Dude shakes his head. "Anyway, listen. I was just telling René here, y'all got your first clown practice tomorrow morning, nine AM sharp, in the rodeo arena. Do not be late. And be sure to wear your running shoes. If you don't have any, we can provide you some. All right, now consolidate those rocks," Rudy Dude drives away.

"I told him you forgot your rake too," Floyd says.

44

Me and Floyd and Cosmic and Jolly are in the rodeo arena we're standing in the dirt in the middle of the rodeo arena we're standing in a line Rudy Dude's in front of us Rudy Dude is big he's big he's a big big man he's walking back and forth back and forth he's looking at us he's wearing silver sunglasses there's something in his mouth he's spitting he spits it's brown it's on his face his face is big and red his head is big and red there's hair only on the sides of his big red head his shirt is hard it's white and hard he's wearing jeans and boots there are two two boxes behind him one box is short it's brown it's filled with clothes the other box is wood and tall it's tall it says 'the outhouse' in big black letters on the top it has targets on it on the sides the targets are painted on the sides it has four wheels the tall wood box has wheels.

"All right, Jolly, ladies, listen up," Rudy Dude says. "I know you'd rather be consolidating rocks, but mid-term week is upon us. Jolly, Cosmic, you two been here before; you know what I'm talking about. Now's the time when ranch hands such as yourselves start into clown practice, once a week for five weeks, in preparation for the term-end rodeo. Jolly. Tell these two retards what a clown does."

"Yessir. Okay, clown's number one job is to protect the bull rider, and the way he does that is a couple of ways. First he, two of them...there are four clowns. Two clowns stand on both sides of the bull chamber when the rider's sitting on the bull in there; the other two are out in the field. One stands out there ready, the other one's called the barrel man, he's inside the barrel and pops out. I'm the barrel man. Then, once the bull rider's going, out in the ring, and he gets thrown off, and he's on the ground, the clowns run around and distract the bull so the rider can get up and get out of the ring safe. Oh, and if the rider gets tangled up with the bull, the clowns have to get him untangled. And if the rider's hurt, the clowns that are not doing anything with the bull have to help him. And if another clown's hurt, they have to help him too. That's it. That's what clowns do. It's real dangerous."

"Yeah, that's right. That is what clowns do. And yes, it is dangerous. Thank you, Jolly," Rudy Dude says. "Now but there is one more thing we need to add to that. Anybody want to guess what it is?"

Floyd types. "However much it pains me to respond to any inquiry of yours, my desire for a complete answer is overriding."

"All right, René. But let's dispense with the goddamn overtures. Just spit it out."

"Be entertaining and funny. That's the other thing clowns do."

"Well what do you know? That is correct. And it's funny you should say that..." Rudy Dude walks over to the box with targets on it. "Because this year *you*, René, are going to be the goddamn funniest and most entertaining barrel man in the history of Dude Ranch."

"Hey, wait a minute, Rudy," Jolly says. "I'm the barrel man, I'm always the barrel man. You always say, I'm the smallest and the most agile, and..."

"Jolly," Rudy Dude says pointing at him. "Do not worry. There are going to be *two* barrelmen this year: traditional - that's you - and non-traditional, that's René. Try to understand, son, that on account of René's special *handi-capability*, this term we have been blessed with this unique comic opportunity."

"Yessir. Sorry sir."

"All right. Now, ladies and gentlemen, let me introduce you to the world's first, and so far only, outhouse clown barrel. It's called 'the outhouse' because that's exactly what it is, an old outhouse. The conversion was executed thanks to a bunch of Mexicans here at the Ranch. They sawed three feet off the bottom of it, mounted it on wheels, and painted it up all nice and pretty, as you can see. And they put a little window on the front so René can see where he's going.

"But probably the most important thing is, they modified it so it fits perfectly right down on top of Old Smokey. Yeah, that's right," Rudy nods he nods. "You get the picture now." He claps one time. "All right, well, time's a wasting. You three get over here and get into some of these dresses and wigs. You'll get official clown suits for the rodeo, but you must wear these for now. This is fixin' to be a real practice, right now. Your colorful outfits are essential in distracting the bull and protecting the riders. The riders are the Ranch's very own graduating senior boys, the cream of the new West Texas bull-riding crop. So, once you get dressed, get the outhouse up on that platform over there and drop it down over René. I'll show you how to secure it to Old Smokey here in a minute. Hey! Carlos!" Rudy Dude yells behind us. "You got me a bull ready in that bull chamber? Carlos!"

"Yeah, Rudy!" Carlos calls back.

There's banging it's coming from the bull chamber there's banging in the bull chamber.

"Well go on," Rudy says, "get dressed."

Me and Cosmic and Jolly put on dresses we put on wigs Jolly says, "I'll be the barrel man, back in the field. You two start up at the bull chamber then run out after he's released."

"Dude, I usually just like, stay over against the rail," Cosmic says he's talking to me. "You'll get boo-ed, but it's like, way better than getting skewered and gored."

We push the outhouse to the platform we lift it up onto the platform Floyd doesn't come he doesn't come with us.

"René! René! Goddammit!" Rudy Dude says he goes and pushes Floyd to the platform.

We lift the outhouse up we hold it over Floyd we let it down. "This is bullshit," Floyd says he's inside the outhouse.

"All right, here," Rudy Dude says he kneels. "See these latches? Snap them all down like so." He snaps the latch. "Got it?"

"Yeah, we got it," Jolly says. "Let's go."

Me and Cosmic are standing up near the bull chamber the bull's behind the gate he's going to come out the gate Cosmic's moving his legs up and down up and down there's banging the bull's banging in the bull chamber he's banging on the gate that's where he's going to come out he's big and brown he's going to come out he has big horns I turn around Floyd's in the outhouse the outhouse is still Jolly's gone there are two barrels where's Jolly Rudy Dude's gone he's gone Rudy Dude's gone too.

"All right," Rudy Dude says he says he's coming through

the speakers I don't see Rudy Dude where's Rudy Dude he says, "First couple runs are rider-free, okay. Main thing is, distract the bull. Make him run after you. Practice your running skills. Use the rails to escape. The object is to grab the flag off the bull's neck. Jolly!" I turn around Jolly stands up he's in a barrel he's in a barrel. "Show 'em how it's done. Carlos, Ready? Okay. Five, four, three, two, one, gate!"

The gate opens the bull comes out the bull comes out he's jumping up and down up and down he's kicking he's running he's running I run I run I run to the rail I jump on the rail the bull comes toward me I jump over the rail.

"All right. That's not it, Birdsong," Rudy Dude says he's talking to me. "You got to stay in there and let him run after you some, then jump on the rail. Only jump over if you absolutely have to. Don't be a pussy. Now get back out there."

Cosmic's standing inside the rail he's inside the rail Carlos goes up to him Cosmic climbs on the rail he climbs over the rail he's back back in the arena he's in the arena with the bull the bull runs to the middle the outhouse is in the middle he puts his head down he rams the outhouse the outhouse falls over it falls on its side.

"Okay, now, get out there and flip that goddamn thing back upright and tell René to keep moving," Rudy Dude says Carlos is in the arena he's running. "Come on!" Carlos says he grabs Cosmic's wrist Carlos pulls Cosmic Cosmic falls over I'm running I run to the outhouse Jolly is jumping up and down jumping up and down running side to side running in front of the bull the bull is just standing now no now he's running he's running he's running he goes after Jolly.

Me and Carlos pick up the outhouse we push it back

upright Rudy Dude says, "Now drive, René, goddammit, drive!" Floyd drives he drives the outhouse the outhouse goes it stops it goes again the bull turns around he stops chasing Jolly he chases the outhouse Floyd drives away the bull rams the outhouse it wobbles it stays up it keeps going it goes faster the bull runs beside it he rams it again it wobbles it stays up it keeps going wobbling Jolly runs over he runs up to the bull he runs next to the bull he's grabbing at something he grabs something yellow he pulls it he jerks it it comes off the bull Jolly yells something he yells at the bull I run over to Jolly I yell at the bull I yell at the bull too.

"That's it, Birdsong. Get in there," Rudy Dude says. "Get him off the outhouse. You and Jolly get him off the outhouse."

The bull rams the outhouse it wobbles it stops it stays up it keeps going I run with Jolly I yell at the bull I jump up and down the bull rams the outhouse the outhouse falls over the bull stops he stops he turns he turns he looks at me he starts walking he's walking toward me I turn I start running I run away I turn around the bull is running he's running behind me I get to a barrel I get behind it.

"Yeah. Hell yeah, Birdsong. That's it," Rudy Dude says.

The bull stops he charges he charges the barrel he hits it it flies up up in the air it's gone he charges me he hits me I go in the air I land in the dirt Jolly's in front of me the bull chases Jolly I crawl to the rail I pull myself over Rudy Dude says, "All right! That is it, Birdsong!" Carlos and Jolly do something the bull goes away Floyd's in the outhouse it's still on its side the wheels are spinning I stay where I am.

Carlos comes over. "Way to get in there, guy. Good job," he says. "You okay? You're holding your ribs."

"My, my side hurts," I say.

"But you're okay."

"Yes, yes, I think so."

"No horn?"

"No, no, no horn."

"All head. Bueno, bueno. That's muy bien. Probably bruised a rib or two, but that's all in a day's work out here, hombre, all in a day's work."

Carlos stands up he waves. "All good here!" He climbs over the rail he's in the arena he runs he runs to Jolly Jolly's next to the outhouse they push it back upright Carlos runs to the bull chamber Jolly runs to his barrel gets in his barrel he stands there he waits.

"All right, Birdsong, hop up and get back in there. Go on," Rudy Dude says I stand up. "Where's Cosmic? Cosmic, wherever you are, get your pussy-ass back out in the arena, now. Carlos. Another bull, please señor. Five minutes."

45

Floyd runs into the back of the elevator we go up the doors open we go out we turn we head to the room.

"Whoa there boys," Nurse Cannary says she's behind her desk she stands up. "Where do think you're going?"

We stop Floyd's pointed toward the hallway.

"What, y'all aren't even going to say 'hi' to little old me today?"

We say, "Hi."

Nurse Cannary puts her hands on her hips. "Floyd, turn and look at me."

Floyd turns toward her.

"Aren't you forgetting something?"

"I don't know. Clown practice was hard. I'm tired. I just want to get some rest."

"But Floyd, you have to get cleaned up properly, and how are you supposed to get cleaned up properly if you don't take your vitamin?"

"I'd really rather not tonight, if it's all the same to you."

"It most certainly is not all the same to me, Floyd. Now." She holds up a needle she taps it. "You must take your vitamin. It is not an option. It's a mandatory component of your rehabilitation. So you can come over here and take it like a man, or I can chase you down the hallway, but one way or the other, I'm going to stick you, and we are going to get cleaned up properly." Nurse Cannary opens her eyes real big.

Wayne drives over to Nurse Cannary. "Atta boy," she says she sticks the needle in his arm. "Okay, see you shortly."

We go to the room.

I take a shower I get out I get dressed Nurse Cannary knocks I open the door she comes in we get Floyd into the shower I get into bed I close my eyes the shower comes on.

Nurse Cannary opens the bathroom door I open my eyes. "Harris," she says, "I'm going to wash Wayne's pee pee here in a few minutes. You're welcome to come in and watch."

"Okay," I say I go to sleep.

46

Me and Floyd are in the rodeo arena parking lot we're consolidating rocks Rudy Dude drives up he stops he gets out of his truck.

"All right, goddamnit," Rudy Dude says. "Stop. Stop raking rocks for one second. Jesus shit. And I was so proud of y'all for your work yesterday too." He shakes his head he stops. "But I know, I *know* it was you two motherfuckers defaced the rodeo college parking lot sign."

Floyd types.

"No, stop. Stop fucking typing, René!" Rudy Dude says.

"We did not deface the sign, we corrected it," Floyd says.

"Shut the fuck up!"

"I did it, I did it," I say, "I took took the paint from the storage barn."

"*You* did it. You *took took* the paint from the storage barn."

"Yes, yes, I did. I, I painted the sign."

"All right. Tie the towrope to your girlfriend's golf cart. When you done that, get in the back of the truck."

"Mr. Dude, Mr. Dude, Floyd didn't do it, he did didn't do it."

"What the fuck do you take me for, a goddamned idiot? Tie that shit up and get in the truck."

I get the rope the cell phone rings it rings in my pocket.

"What the hell was that shit?" Rudy Dude says he puts his hand in his pocket. "It's not mine. Which one of you faggots has got a cell phone out here?"

"It's, it's mine. Doc Holiday gave it to me. It's, it's for emergency."

"Oh really? All right. Well go ahead, answer it."

I take the phone out of my pocket it says, 'Nurse Cannary Calling...' I put the phone to my ear. "Hello."

"Hi, Harris. How are you, darling?" It's Nurse Cannary. "Okay."

"Well, what are y'all doing? What are you boys up to?"

"Working, consolidating rocks."

"Ooh, sounds like fun. Is Wayne available? Could you put him on the line for me?"

"Okay." I look at Rudy Dude

Rudy Dude nods.

I push the button I put the phone in Floyd's lap.

"Wayne? Honey? You there?" Nurse Cannary says.

"Hello," Floyd says.

"There you are. Are you busy? Because things are pretty slow around here, and I was just thinking, why don't you come back to the room for some lunch a little early today? I'm lonely."

Floyd starts to drive away Rudy Dude opens his door Nurse Cannary says, "Wayne, honey, what'd I tell you about driving and talking on the phone?" Floyd stops. "Well, come on, then. What do you say, big dubbya? Don't hold out on little old me."

"You don't understand, Mar'...I have to work. I'm very busy right now."

It's quiet.

"No. You're wrong, Wayne. I *do* understand. I

understand you want me to start giving it to that big-dicked dude-brother of yours. Oh, Wayne, when I peeped out the door the other day and saw he was beating off...Mm, Mm, you would not have believed the size of that boy's cock. God, I've been so anxious to get another look at that thing. I was hoping to get him into the shower with us last night when I was fucking you, but..."

"No no," Floyd says.

"All right, that's enough," Rudy Dude says he comes over to me and Floyd he comes fast. "Give me that thing."

"What?" Nurse Cannary says. "Who is that? Who's there? Wayne?"

Rudy Dude takes the phone out of Floyd's lap he throws it it flies through the air it lands in the parking lot it lands far away.

"Holy shit," Rudy Dude says he shakes his head. "All right, finish tying him up and let's go. Come on, hurry up. God almighty." He gets in his truck.

I tie the rope to the snowplow I get in the back of the truck Rudy Dude puts the truck in gear Floyd jerks forward dust goes all over Floyd we drive to the sign we we stop Floyd rolls forward he hits the back of the truck Rudy Dude leans out the window he yells, "Take the paint and the brush and the stencil that's back there and put that sign back the way it was. Go on, get to it."

I get the paint and the brush and the stencil I get out of the truck stencil's a thin sheet of material with a shape cut out of it that is marked on a surface when paint or ink is applied I go over to the sign Rudy Dude puts the truck in gear he drives he's pulling Floyd dust is going all over Floyd Rudy Dude drives in circle he stops he stops Floyd rolls forward he skids he doesn't hit the truck Rudy Dude leans out the window he says, "Me and René's fixin' to go round in a circle like this here for a little bit. Kill some time. You give me a holler when you get done. We'll come over and check your work. You'll do it as many times as it takes to get it right. Got all day. I'm sure René won't mind." He turns around to Floyd. "Ain't that right, René?" He turns back at me. "Okay. Bye."

I hold up the stencil I paint the word 'lot' back on the sign I wave to Rudy Dude he drives over Floyd's covered in dust his eyes are closed his mouth is closed Rudy Dude gets out of the truck.

"Pretty good there, Pablo," Rudy Dude says. "Look it, though. You got to clean up them edges. See here." He gets up close to the sign he points. "There's little splotches of paint here and there that need to come off, okay. So here." He stands up he reaches into his pocket. "Take my pocketknife and pick that shit off of there, excise that shit." I take the knife. "Come on, René. Couple more times around." Rudy Dude gets in the truck he drives off with Floyd.

I finish I wave to Rudy Dude he says it's okay I get in the truck he says, "Now y'all are really going to move mountains." He laughs.

He drives to the big mountain of rocks behind the hayloft and storage barn he gets out I get out I untie Floyd I get a rag from the barn I clean off Floyd's face.

"Well ain't that sweet," Rudy Dude says. "Whenever you're done hand-washing your girlfriend's face, you two come on over here." He goes he stands on the other side of the mountain of rocks I finish cleaning up Floyd we go over to Rudy Dude.

"All right," Rudy Dude says. "See this circle." He points

with his toe there's a circle it's painted onto the dirt. "See how it goes all the way around yonder and back around over here? What I want y'all to do is...What y'all are *going* to do is move the mountain of stones from over there to inside this circle; you're going to move it from where it is, into here. And I want it done by the end of the term. If it's not done by the end of the term, I draw another circle and you move the mountain there. Shovels and wheelbarrows are in the barn. No lunch break today. Get started." Rudy Dude gets in his truck he drives away.

I go into the storage barn Floyd waits outside I grab a shovel there's no wheelbarrow I turn around it's on the other side of the barn it's by the hay bales it's a mountain of hay bales I walk toward it something moves something moves inside the mountain inside the hay bales I stop I raise the shovel I keep on going I stop David Hill and Rachel Hill walk out of the mountain of hay bales they come out of the mountain of hay.

"Whoa there, cowboy," David Hill says. "Easy with that shovel." I put down the shovel they're covered in hay. "Rachel and I were just back there counting bales for a corral delivery, okay. We got some hungry horses over there." Rachel smiles.

"Okay," I say.

They walk out of the barn.

I walk up to the mountain of hay bales I go around the mountain of hay bales I go where David and Rachel Hill came out there's a room behind the hay bales there's a room under the mountain of hay bales there's a secret room inside the mountain of hay I turn around I put the shovel in the wheelbarrow I go outside.

"What the hell was that," Floyd says.

"David and Rachel Hill," I say.

"I know that. What were they doing in there."

"Counting bales of hay for the corral, they said counting bales of hay for the corral."

"Counting bales of hay."

"For the corral. They have hungry horses over there. Hey Floyd, Floyd? Did you know? There a secret room in in there? There's a secret room under the mountain of hay."

47

We're in the elevator me and Floyd are in the elevator the doors open we go into the infirmary we go into the lobby of the infirmary there's an old lady an old lady sitting behind the desk she looks up. "Well hello, boys," she says.

"Hi," I say.

Floyd says, "Where's Nurse Cannary."

"Was she the last nurse you had up here? I'm sorry, I don't know." I walk over to the desk Floyd follows a little way. "Doc Holiday took me on just today, kind of short notice. He didn't tell me much about who I'm replacing."

"So Nurse Cannary's not coming back," Floyd says.

"Well, Doc Holiday did hire me on full-time, so I assume not. I am Nurse Oakley, but please, you two call me Anne-Marie. You must be Wayne." Floyd doesn't say anything. "And Harris."

"Yes, yes ma'am."

"Great. Well, shall we go and get cleaned up before your meeting with Doc Holiday then?"

Floyd turns and drives down the hall.

"I, I usually take a shower first," I say. "I don't need any help."

"That's fine, Harris. I'll be down shortly."

We go into the room I take off my boots. "It's because Nurse Cannary called, called on the phone today, isn't it,

Floyd? When we were in the parking lot? And and Rudy Dude was there, isn't it, Floyd?"

Floyd types. "I'm sure we'll talk about it later, Harris, with Doc, okay."

I take a shower I get dressed Nurse Oakley comes I get Floyd into the shower Nurse Oakley's old she wears a big black bathing suit she turns on the water I leave the bathroom she's going to wash Floyd's penis.

I go to the window cars and trucks are in the big field they're parked in the big field people are walking between the cars they're under a tent in the field they're wearing orange vests some of them go into the mountains.

I go in the bathroom I get Floyd out of the shower I get him dressed Nurse Oakley leaves I go to the window. "Floyd," I say, "look. Look at all the cars, they're parked in the big field."

Floyd comes to the window. "Must be the Geener search crew. Guess he didn't go home after...Oracle, what is a field, please."

I say all the songs for field there are twenty-one.

"Numbers one and four again, please, Oracle."

"One is an area of open ground. Two is an expanse of something."

"An area of open ground," he says. "And a parking lot is what again."

"An open area of ground in which people can park their automobiles."

"Harris, what is the difference between an open area of ground and an area of open ground."

"I, I don't know, Floyd."

"Shit."

"What is it, Floyd?"

WINTER PARK

"Well, I hate to say it, Harris, but if there is no difference, we owe the Ranch an apology."

48

Doc Holiday opens the door me and Floyd go into his office Floyd stops on the carpet Doc Holiday sits down in his chair I sit on the couch Doc Holiday crosses his legs he puts his pad on his lap he breathes out he uncrosses his legs he leans forward a little he looks down at the floor he says, "Well." He sits back he looks up at us. "Big day. As I'm sure you already know, Nurse Cannary's no longer with us. It's a hard loss, especially given the circumstances...And you two fellows have gotten into some trouble of your own, as well, haven't you?" Doc Holiday looks at the rug he looks at his shoe he looks up up at me. "Harris, care to comment?"

"I, it's, it's because of she, on the phone today. Rudy Dude was there. That's why she's gone."

"Nurse Cannary? Yes, Harris. In many ways, yes. But if you would, please, back up and fill me in. Start from the beginning. Where were you and Wayne? What were you doing?"

"Me, me and Floyd were in the rodeo arena parking lot. We were consolidating rocks. Rudy Dude drove up. He got mad. He got mad at us for painting that sign. The phone rang." Floyd types. "It was..." I say.

"We thought we were correcting it," Floyd says.

"Hold up a second, hold up a second, Harris," Doc Holiday says. "So Wayne, obviously you weren't kidding last time when you said that sign would have to be changed."

"No, I wasn't kidding. I thought it was incorrect the way it was, and when something is incorrect, it's false, and false things should be made true. The problem is, I just discovered that the rodeo college parking lot is, in fact, a parking lot. Now I can no longer justify painting the sign. Harris, we did not correct it; we just defaced it, and for that I am sorry, and I am prepared to make an apology to the Ranch. Harris, I am also sorry for getting you into trouble, for nothing. I should've thought the problem through more carefully."

"That's okay, Floyd. I, I don't mind."

"I definitely think submitting a formal apology to the Ranch is a good idea," Doc Holiday says he writes on his pad he looks up. "You'll both want one on your records. Wayne, without getting too far afield here, I'm interested in your reasoning. What led you to change your mind about the sign?"

"Despite a cosmetic difference in word order, there appears to be no material difference between one of the essences of field, an area of open ground, and the first part of the essence of parking lot, an open area of ground. If there's no material difference, then the term field can be substituted for the terms open area of ground in parking lot so that the essence of parking lot becomes a field in which people can park their automobiles then there's nothing to prevent us from substituting for field another of field's relevant and applicable essences an expanse of something which gives us the following valid revised essence of parking lot an expanse of something in which people can park their automobiles and the rodeo college parking lot is definitely that, so..."

Doc Holiday puts his hand under his chin he pinches his skin he pinches the skin under his chin on his neck he says, "Wayne, that is such a...beguiling analysis. We're going to have to push on, but I really would like to sit down with you sometime and try to understand exactly what it is you're talking about. I really would. Is that something you'd be interested in doing?"

"I suppose."

"I'll talk to Nurse Oakley. We'll see if we can set something up for next week." Doc Holiday pinches his neck he turns to me he drops his hand. "Harris," he says, "how do *you* feel about what you did to the sign, and getting caught?"

"I painted the sign. I, I painted it, we fixed it. Rudy Dude got mad. I don't like it when Rudy Dude gets mad. He pulled Floyd with a rope. I got the brush and the paint and the stencil. Rudy Dude pulled Floyd, with a rope, in a circle. He pulled Floyd, with a rope, in a circle, behind his truck. Dust went all over Floyd, all over Floyd. I don't like it when Rudy Dude gets mad. I painted the sign back, I painted it back. I used a stencil. I painted 'lot' back on the sign. Rudy Dude stopped the truck. Floyd had had dust in his eyes, he had dust in his mouth, he had dust all over him."

Doc Holiday writes on his pad he looks at me. "Anything else?"

"Yes, yes, we went to the mountain, the mountain of rocks. Rudy Dude said to move the mountain of rocks to the other circle. I like moving the mountain of rocks, I do like that."

Doc Holiday laughs. "You're a hard man to punish." He laughs some more. "But now, Harris...Let me ask you something, Harris." He sits forward. "If Floyd jumped off a fifty-story building, would you follow him? Would you jump too?"

"Yes, yes. Floyd, he's my dude-brother."

"Okay, no, see, Harris. Listen to me, carefully. Dude-brothers, while they make a lot of decisions together and do a lot things together, they also make a lot of decisions and do a lot of things apart, independently. You understand?"

"Yes, yes, I understand."

"Floyd is smart, Harris, and I can see you look up to him, but I want to encourage you to start thinking for yourself and making some of your own decisions, okay?"

"Okay."

"All right, let's get back to...where were we?" Doc Holiday looks at his pad he looks up. "Oh yes, Nurse Cannary called on the cell phone. Harris, please continue. What happened when Nurse Cannary called on the cell phone?"

"Nurse Cannary called. She called for Floyd. She said for Floyd to go back to the room. He said he couldn't. He said he had to work. She got mad. She said cock. Cock is straw, hay, or grain, piled in the shape of a cone. She said fucking. I've heard fucking. There's no song for fucking. Rudy Dude grabbed the phone. He threw it a long way."

Doc Holiday writes on his pad. "Very good. Thank you. Okay, first of all..." He puts his pen down he looks up. "Harris, we can't go any further, constructively, until we've cleared up a few things about the birds and the bees, had the talk," he does something with his fingers, "as it were. Are you ready?"

"Yes, yes."

"All right, listen up, Harris. A cock, a cock is a penis. When Nurse Cannary said cock on the phone, she meant pee

pee, penis." He points to his pee pee. "And fucking? Fucking is sex, sexual intercourse. Now, I know you know what a pee pee is, what a penis is. Do you know what sexual intercourse is?"

I ask it comes into my head sexual intercourse is...

"What? What are you looking at Wayne for, Harris?"

"I, the Oracle knows what it is. Floyd, Floyd told me to only be the Oracle if he asked me to. Is it okay if I answer, Floyd?"

"Yes, of course, of course," Floyd says.

Doc Holiday makes a note on his pad. "Wayne, we're going to come back to this...and Harris, case in point, right? Please, *please*, try and forget about Floyd for a minute and tell me what *you* think. I want to know what you, and the Oracle, I guess, know. Do you know what sexual intercourse is?"

"Yes. It's an act carried out for reproduction or pleasure involving penetration."

"Right. But now, in order to be perfectly clear, it means penetration of the man's penis into the woman's vagina, and in this case, Wayne's penis into Nurse Cannary's vagina."

"That's washing the penis," I say. "That's what Nurse Cannary was doing. She was washing Floyd's penis. That's what they called it, washing the penis, the pee pee."

"Okay, now Harris. They called it washing the penis because they did not want you to know what they were *really* doing." Doc Holiday writes on his pad he looks up. "But Harris, when you saw Wayne's penis going into and out of Nurse Cannary's vagina, you saw them fucking, having sexual intercourse."

"She was masturbating his penis with her vagina too. I did masturbation. Masturbation is the stroking of the genitals for sexual pleasure. She was doing that with Floyd's penis."

"Well, not exactly, Harris, because stroking in that case means using the hand, usually your own hand."

"Stroking, stroking is twenty-seven things..."

"That's good, that's okay, Harris. Just trust me. When the penis is massaged by the vagina the act goes beyond mere masturbation into sexual intercourse."

"Purely consensual intercourse," Floyd says.

Doc Holiday turns to Floyd. "Is that so?" He turns back to me. "I'm sorry, Harris. Are we good, for the moment, on this? If we're good, I want to..."

"Yes, yes," I say.

"Okay. Wayne, did Nurse Cannary give you something to produce your erections? Did she inject you with something before getting into the shower? Come on. Remember, it's strictly confidential in here."

"Yes," Floyd says.

"Right. Now, I happen to know that was Viagra." Doc Holiday looks at me. "Viagra causes erections, Harris. It makes your penis get hard, for sexual intercourse." He looks at Floyd. "Did you always agree to those injections, Wayne? *Explicitly* agree to those injections?"

"You didn't agree yesterday, Floyd. You said you didn't want your vitamin yesterday, Floyd. She made you take it anyway."

"Is that true, Wayne?"

"Yes, but..." Doc Holiday puts his hand up Floyd stops typing.

"Wayne, please. Yesterday Nurse Cannary injected you with Viagra against your will then stripped off your clothes, put you in the shower, and, for all intents and purposes, raped you. It follows, from your own admission, that she raped you yesterday."

"It was Harris' admission."

"You corroborated it, Wayne."

"Yes, well, who's to say but me whether I changed my mind in the middle of it; maybe I did, and she was right; maybe, in the end, I didn't know it, but deep down I really wanted to fuck; and even if I didn't, maybe I'm willing to suffer a fuck or two against my will in order to get...any at all. For Christ's sake, put yourself in my shoes, Doc. I'll take anything I can get, even if I don't want it."

"I understand, Wayne, but now, you put yourself in the Ranch's shoes. The Ranch can't have a nurse who, during the scope of, and by virtue of the power vested in her title, systematically takes advantage of a paraplegic patient by pumping him full of Viagra and fucking him in the shower. I'm sure they'd be happy to hear that the sex was consensual – even though we now know not all of it was – but it wouldn't matter, Wayne. Nurse Cannary had to go."

"That's fine. Now I may never have sex again, ever. Where am I going to find another girl who wants, or is even willing to have sex with a fucking paraplegic."

"Look at the bright side, Wayne. First, you got some good sex. It's past now, but it did happen. It didn't have to happen, but it did, and that's a good thing. Second, your penis works. It didn't have to, but it does, and that's a good thing. Third, and this is only an opinion, so take it for what it's worth, but there was one Nurse Cannary who liked fucking you as you are, so there are probably others. It's all about your attitude at this point, Wayne.

"Did you ever hear the story about the woman who was born with no arms and no legs? God, she was nothing but a torso. And yet, and yet, Wayne, because she was in touch with some sort of...power, or vision, she got married, had a bunch of sex with a four-limbed man, and had two four-limbed kids. And, by all appearances anyway, she is, and they are happy."

"What...that's a freak show, though," Floyd says.

"Well, may be, but that didn't stop her from taking what she could get, and that hasn't stopped you either, Wayne...so far anyway."

Doc Holiday stands up he walks to the window he looks out. "Wayne," he says, "what are you going to do, man? What are you going to do with the rest of your life?" He turns around. "What do you want to be when you grow up?"

Floyd doesn't say anything he's quiet Doc Holiday comes back he sits down.

Floyd types. "I want to be a philosopher. I've been thinking about it a lot lately, a lot, and I know, that's what I want to be, a philosopher."

"Want to be?" Docs Holiday laughs. "Wayne, a philosopher is something you most certainly already are. But so what do you mean? You want to get a Ph.D. and work as a philosophy professor at a university, write philosophy books?"

"I don't know. Yes, I guess so, if that's what you do."

"Well, if you want to make philosophy an occupation rather an avocation, that's what you do."

"I've already started writing a dissertation, in my head. I need a printer."

Doc Holiday pinches his neck under his chin. "Yes, yes you do...Wayne, I'll see what I can do about getting you a printer, right away. Seems like, with that keyboard, there'd be an output handy. But, so I assume this dissertation involves the sort of linguistic analyses you've been demonstrating recently? You might actually go ahead and tell me a little more about it now, if you like. Do you mind, Harris?"

"No, no, I don't mind. I'm helping Floyd with it, I'm helping him as Oracle."

"Ah, right, of course," Doc Holiday says.

"It's called 'Parking Lot'," Floyd says. "The Oracle tells us that a parking lot is an open area of ground in which people can park their automobiles. This is what a parking lot really is, this is the essence of the thing, in the world, that the term 'parking lot' is supposed to refer to. The problem is that the essence of parking lot and the essences of the things that are constitutive of a parking lot have, until now, gone unexamined. We have a unique opportunity to change that. So, the immediate purpose of the dissertation will be to establish, by mapping out its constituents and how they relate to one another, what a parking lot really is, and to correct misuse of the term, if any. The more ambitious purpose is to establish a discipline of study dedicated to establishing what all things really are, and to correcting misuse in all terms, wherever it may occur. I'm thinking of calling the misuse of terms, Floyd's Misnomerism, our first case of which I thought we had with parking lot, but...it may turn out that, with regard to misonomerism, the project is more preventative than corrective. It's too early to tell."

"Wow," Doc Holiday says.

"In any case, I have in mind that the dissertation will be in four main sections, not including introduction and conclusion. The first will be, What is an automobile? We have to know just what sorts of thing parks in parking lots. I mentioned this subject last time and have it pretty well thought out. The second will be, What is an open area of ground? We talked a little bit about this earlier today. I am currently working very hard on this section. It's complex. It deals with three major terms, open, area, and ground, and their correspondent essences, jointly and severally. The third is, What is can? Or What can can be? I have not started on this section. Interestingly, though, I do know that can has two simultaneously active essences when it is employed within the essence of parking lot: the first has to do with physical possibility; the second, with moral and legal possibility. These two cans should help limit what a parking lot can be. The fourth is, Miscellanea, in which I deal with the essences of the remaining material terms of the essence of parking lot: parking, lot, in, people, park, and their."

"Wow," Doc Holiday says again he writes on his pad he looks up. "Fantastic, just fantastic, Wayne." He shakes his head.

"Thank you,"

"You're very welcome." Doc Holiday pinches his neck he looks away he looks away for a long time he looks back at Wayne. "Wayne, at the risk of upsetting you, I want to make a few comments, but I want to preface them by assuring you that I think your aspirations to become a professional philosopher are legitimate and realistic. In fact, Wayne, I have enough confidence in your fundamental analytical abilities that I am going to call up a good buddy of mine on the faculty of the philosophy department at Rice University down in Houston. His name is Bob Jogs. Bob and I went to Rice undergrad together a hundred years ago." Doc Holiday smiles. "And I am going to speak with him, on your behalf. I have a feeling that he and the department down there would be very interested in a guy like you, Wayne. Of course, at this point, I realize we, you have no idea the level of your collegiate education, but I assume it doesn't matter to you where in the university process you start, whether you had to start at the beginning, does it?"

"No. I just want to go."

"Well, if you just want to go, then hear me out. I see how this can work, and I want to help you, but you need to know right now, up front, that making this happen is going to mean re-thinking some of your project...two, three major aspects of your project." Doc Holiday looks at Floyd.

"All right, go ahead then. Try me."

"One, if you want to be a professional philosopher, you cannot use an oracle as authority for your premises, as defense, or argument, or proof of the truth of your premises. If you do, you will be the laughing stock of...let's put it this way: the only degree you'll be a candidate for is a BS in new age theology. Two, if you want to be a professional philosopher, you've got to state your premises conditionally; you must introduce them with 'if' and put all your hypotheses in 'If...then' form; you've got to say, 'If a parking lot is such-and-such, then so-and-so follows'. Three, you've got to understand that the real merit, the real magic of your project lies not in establishing the truth of the way things are, based on the authority of some oracle, but in the creativity, agility, precision, the skill with which you are able to derive conclusions from a set of premises, whatever those premises may be. Wayne, it is on the basis of what I perceive to be your capacity for derivation that I will be recommending you to my friend Bob at Rice, not on your ability to consult and interpret an oracle." Doc Holiday sits back.

"But Doc, if I introduce my premises with 'if', I vitiate

the unique authority and revolutionary force of my project. I don't want to do that. I plan on being perfectly forthcoming about the source of my premises because I have complete confidence in the evidence and argument that support Harris' being the Oracle. Initially there will be some skeptics, such as you, but ultimately I think everyone will see that I am right, that he is the Oracle, and that he works with me, and that we are trying to promote a legitimate and ultimately positive philosophical project. With all due respect, Doc, I think when people see what I, the Oracle and I, can offer, they'll capitulate, happily."

Doc Holiday shakes his head he leans forward. "Nope, no. Wayne, I've seen what you and the Oracle have to offer; I haven't capitulated. I'll grant you, Wayne, your argument that Harris is an oracle follows a certain logic, but it does not, in my opinion, provide the best explanation of why Harris is the way he is, why he has access to such an abundance of information. As a professional philosopher, you should be capable of seriously considering more than just one argument or explanation for a particular phenomenon; you must accept the possibility there might be other, better ones. Here, let's see if you can relate to this. It's an argument by analogy.

"Wayne, Harris has a lot in common with a unique and incredible person, a *human being* named Daniel Tammet. Like Harris, Daniel has been subject to epileptic fits. Like Harris, Daniel is a synaesthete: Harris hears what you call the essences of things in song; Daniel perceives each positive number to have its own unique shape, color, and texture. Like Harris, Daniel is capable of incredible feats of mind and memory: he can recite Pi, which is twenty-two divided by seven – an endless number - to twenty-two thousand five hundred and fourteen digits, and he has demonstrated incredible linguistic skills. For instance, Wayne, Daniel learned the Icelandic language, a very complex language, in only one week. People are, understandably, extremely impressed and fascinated by Daniel and his uncanny abilities, but no one considers him to be some sort of Oracle. His abilities derive from the incredible electrical activity in his brain and are probably linked to the epileptic fits he suffered as a child. Do you see my point, Wayne?"

Doc Holiday looks away he pinches neck he looks at us. "Wayne, Harris, this has gone far enough. We need to get to the bottom of this, right now, for both of your sakes, and it occurs to me, Harris, that your sponsor may have all the information we need. Contacting them for information at this point is perfectly legitimate, based on medical need, and the information they provide could very well be critical to both your recoveries. Yes." Doc Holiday nods his head. "Harris, I am going to contact your sponsor and ask them about any particular feats of memory you might have achieved. Specifically, I am going to ask them whether you have memorized a dictionary, and if so, which one. We'll get a copy and compare it to what's in Harris' head. Then we'll know."

"There is no way..." Floyd says.

"Wayne," Doc Holiday points at Floyd Floyd stops typing Doc Holiday stands up he walks back and forth. "Wayne, I don't know what the ultimate merits and implications of treating dictionary definitions as the true, conditionally true premises of your arguments are – we'll have to ask Bob – but that project is a hell of a lot more responsible, interesting, and, I'm sorry, Wayne, a hell of a lot *less* ridiculous than one in which you claim your premises are true because an oracle told you so."

Doc Holiday sits down he looks at Floyd.

"And, perhaps more importantly, Wayne. It spares your dude-brother, Harris here, a lot of trouble. Man, I hate to think, Wayne, that you do not really care about Harris, the human being, that you only tolerate him because you *have to*, because he is inextricably bound up with your precious oracle." Doc Holiday stands up. "No, Wayne, no. Harris is not just a, a *repository*, an unfortunate inconvenience you have to put up with to get what you want. And he is not a puppet, Wayne. You can't *instruct* Harris not to allow anyone else but you to consult with him about the information he has in his head." Doc Holiday walks he stands in front of Wayne. "Wayne, what he talks about with you, and other people, what information he imparts to anyone, is for Harris to decide." Doc Holiday walks he stands in front of me. "Harris, it is up to *you* whether you want to let other people consult with you. Whatever you want to talk to other people about is up to *you*, Harris, okay?"

"Okay."

Doc Holiday walks he walks behind the couch he goes over to the window. "You know what? You know what, Wayne? I think you're jealous. I think you're jealous of Harris, both intellectually and physically." He comes around the couch he sits down he puts his elbows on his knees he looks down there's no hair on the top of his head there's a little brown mark on his head. "But it's understandable." He looks up at Wayne. "It's understandable, Wayne, for a guy in your position. It really is. But you've got to let Harris go, to be what he's going to be." He's talking quietly now he smiles. "He's got to be able to express himself however and whenever and to whomever he wants. And Wayne, finally, you've got to let the Oracle go. You've got to leave him behind. The Oracle's a delusion, Wayne, just a relic from the accident...not to mention he's bad for your career." He laughs. "Trust me." He laughs some more.

"But seriously, Wayne. I know you're probably upset with me right now. You probably think we're operating at cross-purposes, but I want to help you. I really do. In fact, I hope you'll consider me your advisor while you're here, for your dissertation project and for your project to get into Rice. I'm a good editor. I'm good for a strong recommendation. I'm even thinking it would be great experience, great for your CV, if you did a presentation of an excerpt from your parking lot paper in the auditorium towards the end of term. What would you think about that?"

"I don't know."

"All right, well, think about it. There's plenty of time." Doc Holiday stands up Floyd drives toward the door I stand up. "Okay fellows, I'll be in touch, probably next week, about the results of our inquiry with your sponsor, Harris. In the meantime, I'll work on getting you that printer, Wayne." Doc Holiday opens the door. "Oh, and have fun at the dance tomorrow night."

We go back to the room Floyd's quiet.

49

"'Pasamonte, who was anything but meek (being by this time thoroughly convinced that Don Quixote was not quite right in his head as he had committed such a vagary as to set them free), finding himself abused in this fashion, gave the wink to his companions, and falling back they began to shower stones on Don Quixote at such a rate that he was quite unable to protect himself with his buckler, and poor Rocinante no more heeded the spur than if he had been made of brass. Sancho planted himself behind his ass, and with him sheltered himself from the hailstorm that poured on both of them. Don Quixote was unable to shield himself so well but that more pebbles than I could count struck him full on the body with such force that they brought him to the ground; and the instant he fell the student pounced upon him, snatched the basin from his head, and with it struck three or four blows on his shoulders, and as many more on the ground, knocking it almost to pieces. They then stripped him of a jacket that he wore over his armour, and they would have stripped off his stockings if his greaves had not prevented them. From Sancho they took his coat, leaving him in his shirt-sleeves; and dividing among themselves the remaining spoils of the battle, they went each one his own way, more solicitous about keeping clear of the Holy Brotherhood they dreaded, than about burdening themselves with the chain, or going to present themselves before the lady Dulcinea del Toboso.

The ass and Rocinante, Sancho and Don Quixote, were all that were left upon the spot; the ass with drooping head, serious, shaking his ears from time to time as if he thought the storm of stones that assailed them was not yet over; Rocinante stretched beside his master, for he too had been brought to the ground by a stone; Sancho stripped, and trembling with fear of the Holy Brotherhood; and Don Quixote fuming to find himself so served by the very persons for whom he had done so much.'"

Nurse Oakley closes the book she stands up. "Good night," she says I close my eyes she turns out the light she leaves.

50

It's morning it's morning I come out of The Big House Floyd comes out of The Big House I go down the stairs Floyd goes down the ramp I wait for Floyd I wait at the bottom of the ramp Floyd comes down the ramp he drives past me he drives fast I catch up I walk next to him he slows down I wait he speeds up he goes past me we pass the corral Rachel comes out of her bunkhouse a bunch of girls come out of the bunkhouse they follow Rachel me and Floyd stop we stop for them Rachel looks at me she smiles at me Rachel and the girls pass they pass me and Floyd go on.

"Floyd? Floyd?"

"What. What is it, Harris."

"Who, who are you going to dance with, tonight at the dance, Floyd? I'm going to dance with Rachel, Floyd."

"If you haven't noticed, Harris, I won't be dancing with anyone, tonight or any night, ever, and no, no you're not, you're not going to dance with Rachel. Our dance is for ranch hands only, Harris. And listen, I'm sorry, but I don't know if I can talk to you any more right now, not until we get the word from your sponsor on whether you memorized a dictionary or not. I hope you didn't, because if you did...if you did, somehow...that means...You tricked me, Harris..."

"No, no, Floyd, I never..."

"...And even if you didn't trick me outright into thinking

you're the Oracle, Harris, you might've cultivated the misconception, to your advantage, so I would be your friend, because...because, let's face it, Harris, without the Oracle, all you are is a fucking idiot, and being your friend makes me look like a fucking idiot too. It makes us look like two goddamn fucking idiots, Harris, just, like you say, going around doing stuff. Shit. It's fucking unbearable."

"Floyd, I..."

"Shut the fuck up, Harris. We'll see about all this shit soon enough, okay. So just shut the fuck up."

"Okay, Floyd."

Floyd speeds up he drives ahead.

I get the snowplow I get the snowplow out of the storage barn I put it on Floyd's chair he goes around the side of the mountain he pushes rocks into a pile I go back into the storage barn I get the wheelbarrow I get a shovel I come out Floyd's pushing rocks over the ground he's pushing them to the other circle he's losing a lot of rocks they're going off the side of the snowplow I shovel rocks off the side of the mountain I put them in the wheelbarrow Floyd goes to the other side of the mountain Floyd works on the other side of the mountain.

Lunch time comes Floyd goes to The Big House I keep working I shovel rocks I move rocks I move the mountain there's knocking behind me.

"Yoo hoo. Anybody home?" It's a girl it's it's Rachel I stop I stop shoveling Rachel Rachel's wearing a white shirt it's a cowgirl shirt she's wearing blue jeans and boots Rachel's hair is long and dark it's black and purple. "Jeez, Harris," Rachel says. "Working through lunch, huh?"

"Yes, yes ma'am."

"Harris, now you know better than that. You know

better than to call me ma'am. It's Rachel, okay. Now stop that working and come over here and help me out."

I come down off the mountain. Rocks fall down they fall at her feet.

"Sorry, sorry, Rachel." Rachel's shirt her shirt's unbuttoned at the top.

"Don't worry about it, Harris. What I need is a couple of extra bridles for this afternoon's trail ride. We got the whole student group going out this time, so...you want to come in here and help me look for them?"

"Yes, yes, I'll help you look for them."

Rachel walks into the barn. "Well come then, you big dummy."

I follow Rachel in into the barn she walks to the mountain of hay.

"Rachel, the, the bridles are over here, they're over here."

Rachel turns her head she keeps walking. "The ones I'm looking for are over here, Harris. Come on."

I follow her she goes around the wall of hay bales I go around the wall of hay bales she's standing in the little room under the mountain of hay inside the mountain of hay she's unbuttoning buttons on her shirt all the buttons on her shirt I stop my penis moves it moves inside my jumpsuit.

"I found them," Rachel says.

"Where, where are they?"

"Right here. Come here. I'll show you. Come on." Her shirt falls to the ground it falls behind her I walk I walk to her.

"You show me yours and I'll show you mine," Rachel says she unhooks the front the front of her underwear she lets go of it she moves her shoulders back it drops it to the ground she comes up up to me she puts her hand on my penis she holds my penis through my suit her breasts touch my suit. "God, it's true, isn't it."

"What, what?"

Rachel steps back. "All right, shut up and take this stupid suit off." She takes the zipper she pulls it down she reaches in she holds my penis hard. "Take it out. Now."

My jumpsuit falls to the ground she pulls down my underwear they're at my feet they're around my boots my penis gets big my penis gets hard hard she takes my penis in her hand she leans over she puts my penis in her mouth inside her mouth she has my penis in her mouth she looks up she looks down she goes up and down up and down she's sucking sucking on my penis in her mouth she's making noises more and more she's making noises something's happening in my penis it's in my penis something's happening she's pulling down her blue jeans she's pulling down her underwear the sound of gravel and the motor come they come into the barn they come around the hay bales the chair Floyd's chair Floyd is coming Rachel says, "Don't worry, Harris," but Floyd says, "Harris," into the barn around the hay bales. "Harris," he's driving he's driving he's coming in. "Shit!" Rachel says she steps back back she pulls up her underwear she pulls her pants up up. "Go, go!" she says I pull up my underwear I pull up my suit up I zip up my suit my penis hurts I go I leave I leave the room I leave Rachel there I walk into the barn there's Floyd.

"I saw Rudy on the way over here," Floyd says. "He's coming by in a minute to check on our progress." He turns he leaves he goes outside I stand there the sound of Rudy Dude's truck comes into the barn the truck stops outside the barn I walk out of the barn.

51

We wear regular clothes to the dance I wear blue jeans and brown work boots I wear a blue shirt the shirt's got a little pocket on the front me and Nurse Oakley get Floyd into brown pants and brown shoes he wears a green shirt Nurse Oakley wears a long red skirt it goes down to her feet she wears a white shirt it covers her arms and neck we're ready Floyd says, "I'm not going."

"Wayne," Nurse Oakley says.

"I told you, I'm not going." Floyd drives to the window he stops.

"Wayne, I'm surprised at you. I took you for more of ladies' man than that. Now come on. Get it in gear. There will be other girls down there besides me. And you know, it's not only about the dancing; it's about mingling and getting to know the other ranch hands too. So come on, let's go."

"They still haven't found Chip Geener, have they," Floyd says.

"No, no they haven't, Wayne, but we'll keep him in our prayers, won't we?" Nurse Oakley says she looks at me. "All right, Wayne, you old party-pooper, Harris and I will just go, then, but I'm telling you, it's going to be fun."

Nurse Oakley and I go out of The Big House Jackie

Sherwood and her students go by she leads her girls in front of The Big House I stop I watch them they go around The Big House they go behind it they go away.

"The student and instructor dance is at the outdoor amphitheater, Harris," Nurse Oakley says. "The ranch hand dance is in the rodeo college parking lot."

We go to the rodeo college parking lot there's red and blue and green and yellow lights they're they're hanging from the ceiling they're hanging from the metal bars in the ceiling in the corner there's some folding chairs there's a table with a box on it there's a music box on it there's a table with a bowl on it a bowl of red punch on it there's cups there's no one else there me and Nurse Oakley sit down.

Nurse Oakley says, "Harris, would you mind getting me a cup of punch?"

I get up I pour Nurse Oakley a cup of punch I hand it to her she winks. "Don't worry, Harris. It'll pick up."

Rudy Dude and a Mexican girl walk up the Mexican girl's wearing a fancy white dress I stand up.

"Evening, Nurse Oakley, Mr. Birdsong," Rudy Dude says. "This here's Maria, Dude Ranch's very own quinceañera. That means she just turned fifteen, Birdsong, so she's ready to go, if you know what I mean." Rudy Dude laughs Maria looks down. "Maria, this is Nurse Oakley and Harris Birdsong. I asked Maria to come over tonight in order to ameliorate the male-to-female ratio. Now - and thanks to you, too, Nurse Oakley - it's even. Where the hell's Floyd?"

"Said he didn't want to come, Rudy," Nurse Oakley says.

"The hell he did. Where's he at? Up in the..." He points toward The Big House Nurse Oakley nods. "Be right back." He leaves.

"Habla Ingles, Maria?" Nurse Oakley says.

"Oh yes, I speak English."

"Well that is a gorgeous dress, darling? When was your quinceañera?"

"Mi quinceañera? Oh, it's today."

"Today? Congratulations. That's wonderful. But hey, shouldn't you be with your family? Maria, you should be with your family, honey. Please, you go on back home now. I'll deal with Rudy."

"Oh, no Señora. I stay here. This is mi obligación." Maria looks at me.

"Your obligation?" Nurse Oakley says.

"Oh yes. My obligation, mi deber. When Rudy says come, all my family, they explain to me I must go."

"Okay, Maria. If you're sure. But listen. Any time you want to go home, please feel free to do so, okay? Now, Harris, why don't you offer Maria a cup of punch?"

I go over I pour Maria a cup of punch I hand it to her.

"Now show her a seat, Harris."

Maria goes to a chair she sits down I sit down I sit between her and Nurse Oakley.

"Harris, why don't you tell Maria a little bit about yourself?"

I don't say anything.

"Maria, Harris is a ranch hand. He stays in a room in The Big House, in the infirmary, with his dude-brother, Wayne Floyd."

"Yes," Maria says, "Yo sé."

"You know? You and Harris have already met?"

"Oh no. I know he live in The Big House."

"I see. Of course. So Harris, what does a ranch hand do, exactly?"

"Con...consolidate rocks," I say. "Ranch hand

consolidates rocks. I consolidate rocks with a rake. Me and Floyd got in trouble. We move the mountain of rocks now. We move the mountain of rocks, to another circle."

"You're a sort of groundskeeper then?"

A groundskeeper's somebody who maintains a playing field or the grounds of a property. "Yes, yes."

"Is that something you enjoy doing, Harris? Working with your hands?"

"Yes, yes."

"That's good, Harris. Maria..." Nurse Oakley looks around me. "Harris is also a student, or starting next week he's going to be. Harris, I was going to tell you tomorrow, but I don't see any harm in telling you now. Beginning next week you and I are going to start meeting every morning, for class, as it were. We're going to be doing psychology and English at the same time. We're going to learn how to slow down and recognize what we're thinking and feeling, and then we're going to learn how to express what we're thinking and feeling in language, in English. Does that sound good? You'll be a student in the mornings, just like the students here at the rodeo college, and a ranch hand in the afternoons."

"Yes, yes, Nurse Oakley. That sounds good," I say. "Is, is Floyd going to be in class too?"

"Yes and no, Harris. Wayne is going to be in class, but he isn't going to be in *our* class. He is going to be in a different class each morning, with Doc Holiday, to work on philosophy."

"Are, are me and Floyd still going to meet with Doc Holiday together?"

"Actually, no, Harris. We're changing that next week too. Doc thinks that, at this point, you'll each get more out of your sessions with him if you come separately."

Nurse Oakley looks around me. "Maria, what do you do, here at the Ranch?"

"Oh, trabajo en la cocina."

"Are you a cook?"

"No. I washing dishes. My mother, she cooking."

Rudy Dude comes back pushing Floyd he pushes Floyd to us he stops he says, "The others are on their way over. I checked in on them on my way to get René here." He walks over to the table with the music box on it. "And here's your evening's entertainment. You just press this button right here and voilá, an endless parade of delightful dancehall favorites to which you can trip the light fantastic." Rudy Dude laughs. "All right, Nurse Oakley, I will leave these gay festivities in your capable hands at this point and bid you all a good night. So goodnight," Rudy Dude says and leaves.

"Well," Nurse Oakley says, "I guess we'll wait a few minutes for the other..." Laughter comes from the other side of the parking lot it's Cosmic and Jolly and Laura Tate and Sarah Castleberry they walk across the parking lot they walk to us we say, "Hi," everybody says, "Hi."

Cosmic's wearing a red and blue and yellow shirt with flowers all over it he's wearing white shorts and sandals Jolly's wearing blue jeans and a blue long-sleeve shirt he's wearing his boots and his cowboy hat Sarah Castleberry's wearing a blue big lady's dress she's wearing sandals Laura Tate's wearing a tight red shirt and a short blue skirt she's wearing black pointy shoes they make her taller she's smoking a cigarette.

"Oh, hey," Laura says she says to me. "How's your big, boot?" She blows smoke out of her mouth. "You know, the one with the hole in it."

"Laura, honey," Nurse Oakley says, "there's no smoking at this event, okay. Please put that cigarette out."

"Mm," Laura says smoking the cigarette she breathes in. "'Kay, Nurse O'," she says she blows out the smoke she looks at me and drops the cigarette she mashes it into the ground with the toe of her shoe.

Nurse Oakley stands up me and Maria stand up Maria takes my hand Laura looks away.

"Well all right, everybody. Let's strike up the band," Nurse Oakley says she goes over to the music box she presses a button the music comes on she turns it down Laura and Jolly and Cosmic and Sarah talk they laugh they drink punch Nurse Oakley drinks punch she sits down she sits next to Floyd she talks to Floyd she gets up she gets more punch she sits down next to Floyd she talks to Floyd she drinks punch Maria stands in front of me she puts her hands on my shoulders she starts to dance.

"Harris," she says. "I have to tell you somethings, I have to ask you somethings."

"What, what is it, Maria?"

Laura walks up. "May I cut in," she says she pushes Maria Maria steps back. "Sit down, Spica," Laura says she puts her arms around my neck she starts to dance Maria sits down.

"So. Harris," Laura says. "Look it. I know there's no use beating around the bush with you. So, what I want to propose is this: you beat it *in* the bush with *me*." Laura laughs Maria's looking at Laura she's talking to herself and looking at Laura she stands up. "See, rumor has it," Laura says, "you're hung like a horse, and I..."

Maria pushes Laura Laura falls down. "Es mi pareja, puta! Vete! Vete!" Maria says.

"What? You bitch!" Laura says she gets up she heads for Maria I put my arm out I stop her Nurse Oakley comes over.

"Here, here. Come now, girls," Nurse Oakley says. "What's all the excitement about?"

"She stole my partner," Maria says.

"She pushed me down," Laura says.

"Okay, all right, settle down," Nurse Oakley says. "Now. Harris, who, who were you dancing with? Who was your partner, Harris?"

"Maria, Maria."

"All right then. Laura, Maria is Harris' partner. Now leave them be. Go on." Laura says something she walks away. "And no more pushing, Maria, por favor."

"Si, señora, okay."

Laura gets punch she drinks she dances with Jolly Cosmic and Sarah dance too Nurse Oakley gets punch she sits down with Floyd she talks to Floyd.

Maria puts her hands on my shoulders. "I sorry."

"That's, that's okay, Maria."

We dance we go side to side we go in a circle.

"Harris. I have to talk to you, Harris. I have to ask you somethings. Es muy importante." She looks at me. "I sorry. I try to speak English." We turn in a circle. "Harris. I in trouble because my brother. I lose him. Now he is gone, and it's all my fault." She puts her head down she looks up she's crying. "My brother, his name is Pablo. He is ten years old. He just a little boy." She puts her head down.

"What? What happened, Maria?"

She looks up. "He was with me, at the rodeo last term. Papi, he was in the arena, and mamma, she was cooking. I take Pablo to the cotton candy, and when I pay, I lose him. I want to give to him the cotton candy but he gone. He no there, he no there. I look, I look, but I no see nothing. Ay dios mio." She puts her head on my chest she cries. "Oh por favor, Harris, ayúdame, ayúdame, por favor."

"Where, where's Pablo gone, Maria?"

Maria takes her head off my chest she looks at me. "At first, we think Pablo, maybe he get lost in the mountain, maybe he die in the mountain. We talk to Rudy Dude, he say there javelina in the mountain, maybe they eat Pablo. But we don't believe this no more, Harris, we don't believe this because this no is Pablo. No, Pablo, he like to stay close, Harris. My mamma, all my family, we believe Nurse Cannary, she take Pablo at the rodeo last term, at the cotton candy. She take Pablo, she give him to the warden, and the warden, she take Pablo in her house, she lock him in a *cage*."

"Oh," I say Maria cries she cries on my chest.

Maria looks up. "Harris, you remember the warden, she is in the auditorium, on the movie in the auditorium?"

"Yes."

"And the warden, she is talking, but we no can see her?"

"Yes."

"And the warden, she say, 'Come here, Preston', and she speak Spanish and she walk, on the floor, she, she, the, the footsteps, they go away, in the house?"

"Yes."

"And my mamma, in the auditorium, she scream, and the mens, they take her out?"

"Yes."

"Okay, Harris. My mamma, she say she *hear Pablo, in the warden house, she hear the soul of Pablo, in the warden house*." Maria grabs my shirt. "No hay Preston in the warden house, Harris. It's Pablo. That's why mamma, in the auditorium, she scream, Harris. My mamma, she *know* these things, Harris. She *know*."

"But, but Pres'...Preston's a dog, Maria. He's a dog, Maria, isn't he?"

"No. No, Harris. Preston, he no is a dog." Maria shakes her head. "Rudy Dude, he say the same. After the warden was in the auditorium, we go to him, we tell him. He say, Preston, oh he is a dog, or he is a cat, or he is something like that, a pet. He say we crazy, but we no crazy, Harris. Mi tia Rosalía, she was cleaning the warden house, last spring, all the last spring, before the warden stop coming out. No dog. The warden, she has no dog, Harris, no dog, no cat, no nothing, Harris. We tell this too, to Rudy Dude, but still he say we crazy. Rudy Dude, he think *we* are dogs, Harris. He treat *us* like dogs. He no help us, Harris, but you...you help us, Harris. You live in The Big House. You help us get Pablo back, Harris." She puts her head on my chest. "I have to get mi Pablo back, Harris. I am maldita to my familia, Harris."

Nurse Oakley stands up she gets more punch Laura and Jolly and Cosmic and Sarah drink punch they dance they laugh.

"I, I don't, I..."

"Oh, please, Harris. Harris, I do anything you want."

"What, what do mean, Maria?"

"For the...the, the sex." She looks down.

"You, you mean sexual intercourse, Maria?"

Maria looks up. "Si, si, yes, Harris. I do sex with you if you help me...if, if I have to, Harris." She cries.

"No, no, Maria. No sex. You are only a girl. And I have a girlfriend now too, Maria. I have a girlfriend now. Her name is Rachel. We have sexual intercourse, okay? It's okay, see?"

Maria stops dancing she looks up at me. "Harris. I no understand. You help us o no?"

"Yes, yes."

"But you don't want nothing from me, Harris? You don't want the sex?"

"No, no."

Maria puts her head on my chest. "Oh gracias. Dios mio, gracias. Mi familia, they say you have a heart, Harris. Es verdad, es cierto." She looks up she smiles. "You are an angel, Harris, mi angel."

We dance.

"After the warden, she was in the auditorium, and my mamma, she scream, and we talk to Rudy Dude and he don't do nothing, all my cousins, they want to attack The Big House, they want to break the door to the warden house, but my father, he tell them, No, we must use the head. He say, If we use the anger, the violencia, people going to get hurt, people going to die, *Pablo* going to die. He remember to my cousins the boy in the warden story, he die, he die because the people put rocks in the lady house, they use the violence to make her come out. My father, he is a wise man, he make another plan. He say you are the key, Harris. He call you la roca silenciosa, Harris. My cousins, they argue to him, they say, Pero he is el tonto del pueblo, but my father, he say, No, he has a heart of gold y the memory of un gigante, un elefante, he care and he careful. So, Harris, when Rudy Dude tonight, he wants I come to the dance, reconocemos el destino.

"Now I going to tell you what to do, Harris, and you do what I say because my family, we know all the secrets of The Big House, and my father, he make the best plan for you, for Pablo, okay?" She points to her head. "So escúchame bien ahora. You listen to me and you remember, okay?

"Okay, Maria. I will listen. I will remember."

"And you don't tell nobody what I going to say, Harris, okay? Except you amigo, Monty Jolly. You tell him because he going to help you, Harris, okay?"

"Okay, Maria."

"Okay. Only there is one way into the warden house now, Harris: in the shaft for the dumbwaiter, but only you can go up the shaft into the warden house when the dumbwaiter, it is down in the basement because if the dumbwaiter, it is up at the warden house, it block the door to go into the warden house. And the warden, only she control the dumbwaiter. Only she push the button, it come up to her house from the basement. Only she push the button, it go down to the basement. The dumbwaiter, it no stop at the other floor no more, Harris, only the warden floor and the basement floor. You button no work, but still you can get into the shaft on you floor, Harris. You open the door on you floor, you go in, you climb up inside. When the dumbwaiter, it is down, you climb up the ropes, you open the door to the warden house, you go inside the warden house. This how you get in. You understand?"

"Yes."

"But the dumbwaiter, right now it is up at the warden house, Harris. Most time it is up. The warden, she no put it down very much to the basement. Only one time before she did. Last month. It's fill with trash, much, much trash. But Harris, she leave it down, she leave it down for a week. So, it possible we wait another month, Harris, but the warden, she gonna make trash, she gonna to make trash, and she going to put it down in the basement another time, and when she put it down, Harris, you going to have a sign. Mi tia Rosalía, she clean you room everyday, Harris, she going to leave a little rock on you pillow. This mean the dumbwaiter, it down, it mean you can climb up into the warden house in the night, in this night. Comprendes, Harris?

"Yes."

"Bueno. Now, my father, he say you friend, Monty Jolly, *he* climb up the shaft into the warden house, because he small, and he a thief. He very good to go into the warden house. He no get caught, Harris. Also, he do it because he like Rudy Dude, he want to be Rudy Dude friend, he want to help Rudy Dude be the warden.

"But Harris, escuchame. This, this the most important thing, okay? The warden, she must never, *never* know that somebody come into her house. She must *never* know. If she know, she going to kill Pablo, Harris, just like in the warden movie. She going to *kill* Pablo. You understand?"

"Yes, yes. I understand, Maria."

"Okay, so, when Monty Jolly, he inside the warden house, he make no noise. Only he look for something it show, it prove Pablo, he inside the warden house. He look for a toy, clothes, something that is for Pablo, for a ten-year old boy. If he find nothing, he just go out, and he no get caught. But Harris, mi madre, she think he going to find something. She think she hear it in the movie, on the warden table." Maria puts her hand up to her chest she reaches into the top of her dress she pulls out a brown stick it has a brown cup on it the stick has a white string tied to it the string has a brown ball on the end of it she holds it up. "Pablo most favorite toy. It's balero, cup and ball game. He love it, *love* it, Harris, and he have it with him at the rodeo. Pablo balero is this one, exactamente the same this one." She hands me balero. "Take it." I take it. "Now, if you find this, or other thing for Pablo, in the warden house, this is next what you must do, what you *must* do, Harris. Okay? You listen."

"Okay."

"You take the thing to Rudy Dude at Rudy Dude house inmediatamente. Right away you go out from The Big House in the emergency stair, you go down to Rudy Dude house, you show to him this thing, prove to him Pablo inside the warden house. And Harris, if this thing, it's Pablo balero, Rudy Dude, he is happy because he know about Pablo balero, Harris. We tell him before about Pablo balero. If Rudy Dude see Pablo balero, he *know* Pablo inside the warden house, and he call the sheriff because Rudy Dude, he want to be warden very much. The sheriff, then he find the way to bring Pablo home safe. The warden, she go to jail, and the curse, it leave me." Maria shakes her head she stops she puts her hands on my chest she looks at me. "But Harris, there is one more thing you *must* remember, you *not* forget, okay?"

"Okay, Maria."

"You must put this thing, Pablo balero, back in the warden house, right away, same night, before the warden, she wake up. Maybe you take the picture of it or something, Harris, for the proof to the sheriff, but after you show to Rudy Dude, you *must* put it back. Monty Jolly, he must climb back into the warden house, put it back in the warden house just where he find it. Harris, if you no do this, the warden, she know, she know somebody been in her house, and she going to kill Pablo, Harris." Maria puts her head on my chest. "Ay dios mio."

She looks up. "You promise, you promise you help me?"

"Yes, yes. I promise, Maria."

"And all of this, you remember? You won't forget?"

"Yes, Maria. I remember. I remember everything, everything you said is a song. I will never forget."

Maria smiles. "Oh, Harris, it so beautiful." Tears come into her eyes. "When next day, this plan, it's finish..." She wipes her eyes she looks at me. "I come see you. I find you, Harris. You tell me good news, okay?"

"Okay, Maria," I say.

"Ay dios mio. Gracias, gracias, Harris." She hugs me. "I know you help me. I know, I know. I go now, okay. I tell everybody, mi padre, mi familia. They are so happy for this, Harris. Hasta luego, mi pareja. I see you soon." She takes off her shoes she runs across the parking lot she runs out of the parking lot she's gone.

"Uh oh, Harris," Laura says. "What'd you do?"

Part 4

Harris Birdsong

WINTER PARK

52

late summer **2000**

I pick up the last rocks with my hands and put them in the wheelbarrow. I push the wheelbarrow to the new mountain and shovel the rocks onto it. Some rocks fall off the mountain out of the circle. I push them back inside the circle with my boot. Floyd drives toward me. He drives toward me, and I back away. He pushes at the side of the mountain with the snowplow. He goes around the whole mountain of rocks and pushes at the sides with the snowplow. He's making sure all the rocks are inside the circle; he's making sure the whole mountain is inside the circle.

I put the shovel in the wheelbarrow and push the wheelbarrow into the storage barn. I take the broom. I go out of the barn and sweep the open area of ground where the first mountain was. I sweep the dirt. Floyd's driving away. He's driving away from the mountain. He's driving toward the Mexican bunkhouses and the rodeo college parking lot. He disappears.

Nurse Oakley says if I dislike something it upsets me, I am upset by something. If to dislike something is to consider something unpleasant, and if something is unpleasant something it is not pleasing, then to dislike something is to consider something to be not pleasing; and if to be upset by something is to be unhappy because of something, and if to be unhappy is to be not pleased with something, then to be upset by something is to be not pleased with something; and if to consider something to be not pleasing is to be not pleased with something; then, to dislike something is to be upset by something, and Nurse Oakley is right.

Nurse Oakley says if I am very upset I am in pain. If to be upset is to be emotionally distressed, to be very upset is to be very emotionally distressed; and if to be in pain is to be in severe emotional distress; and if to be in severe emotional distress is to be very emotionally distressed; then, to be very upset is to be in pain, and Nurse Oakley is right.

Nurse Oakley says if I am in pain I am really sad, or scared, or angry. If to be in pain is to be in severe mental distress, if distress is mental suffering caused by grief, and if grief is great sadness, then to be in pain is to be in severe mental suffering caused by great sadness; and if to be in severe mental suffering caused by great sadness is to be really sad; then, to be in pain is to be really sad, and she is right.

If to be in pain is to be in severe mental distress, if distress is mental suffering caused by anxiety, and if anxiety is to be in a state of intense fear, then to be in pain is to be in severe mental suffering caused by a state of intense fear; and if to be scared is feeling full of fear; and if to be in severe mental suffering caused by a state of intense fear is feeling full of fear; then, to be in pain is to be scared, and Nurse Oakley's right.

If pain is something that is extremely annoying; and if to be angry is feeling extremely annoyed; and if to have something that is extremely annoying is feeling extremely annoyed; then, to be in pain is to be angry, and Nurse Oakley is right.

I stop sweeping the dirt and go over to the new mountain of rocks. I check the edges. The edges are clean. There are no rocks outside the circle. The whole new mountain of rocks is inside the circle. The new mountain is done.

Nurse Oakley says if I like something I am happy about something. If to like something is to regard something as enjoyable, and if something is enjoyable it is providing pleasure, then to like something is to regard something as providing pleasure; and if to be happy is feeling pleasure; and if to regard something as providing pleasure is feeling pleasure; then, to like something is to be happy about something, and Nurse Oakley is right.

I put the broom in the storage barn and check inside the mountain of hay, but Rachel's not there; she's not there.

Nurse Oakley says I can tell if I really want something because I feel it in my body. She says I feel everything in my body. She says if I really want something I desire something. If to desire something is to want something very strongly; and if to really want something is to want something very strongly; then, to really want something is to desire something, and Nurse Oakley is right.

I walk to The Big House. I go in and take the elevator up. The doors open. I see Nurse Oakley and say hello. She'll be down in a minute. I go down the hall. I open the door. Floyd's by the window. There's a rock on my pillow.

53

I take a shower and get dressed. Nurse Oakley comes down. She and Floyd take a shower. We get Floyd dressed. The phone rings.

"Is somebody going to answer that?" Nurse Oakley says.

I answer it. "Hello."

"Hello, Harris?" Doc Holiday says. "You all in the middle of something?"

"I, I don't..."

"Are you busy?"

"No, no sir. No one is fully occupied in a particular activity."

"Okay, good. Then could you all go ahead and come on down to my office, right now. I know we're not due here for our little fiesta for another twenty minutes, but I've got Bob Jogs at Rice on the other line, and he's...well, anyway, can you all just come on down. Thanks, Harris." Doc Holiday hangs up the phone.

Nurse Oakley, Floyd, and I go down to Doc Holiday's office. He opens the door and smiles. He appears to be in a state of happiness. "Yes, yes, come on in folks," he says. Nurse Oakley, Floyd, and I go in. It smells like food. There's a silver tin, two drink pitchers, some cups and plates, two green and white and red flags on the table by the window. Floyd drives over and stops on the other side of the couch.

Nurse Oakley and I sit on the couch. Doc Holiday stands next to his desk.

"Bob," Doc Holiday says, "still there?"

"Yeah, John, still here," a man's voice says. It comes from a little silver box sitting on Doc Holiday's desk. Doc Holiday turns the box the other way, to face us.

"Okay, Bob, I have here on my end Nurse Anne-Marie Oakley, Mr. Wayne Floyd, Mr. Harris Birdsong."

"Hi everybody," Bob says.

We all say, "Hi."

"Everybody, on speaker phone with us today we have an old college buddy of mine, Professor Bob Jogs. He is the chairman of the philosophy department at Rice University down in Houston. Bob, you were asking me if you'd called at a bad time, but your timing couldn't be better really. We are at the end of the summer term at the ranch, and the four of us were slated to gather in my office for a little end of term Mexican fiesta right about now anyway, so..."

"Well good, that's good," Bob Jogs says out of the little box. "I'm glad."

Doc Holiday looks around. "No margaritas, though," he says. "Nurse Oakley, where's that margarita machine we requested?" Nurse Oakley and Bob Jogs and Doc Holiday laugh.

"Hey, I'm not sure you can call it a fiesta if you don't have margaritas, John," Bob Jogs says. They laugh some more.

"Well, you know how it is. It ain't like the days back at Valhalla," Doc Holiday says.

"No, no. And it's a good thing too," Bob Jogs says.

"Valhalla is name of the bar on the Rice campus. Valhalla's still there, I assume, Bob."

"Oh yeah. The administration threatens to close it down every year, but it never happens. It's a Rice fixture."

"Good to know, good to know." Doc Holiday sits on the edge of his desk. "All right, well, margaritas or no, we do have a lot to celebrate here, Bob. It has really been an incredible term, and, from what I understand, you're about to make it even more incredible. Is that right? Of course, I know it only directly concerns Wayne, but the four of us have become very close over the last few months, like a little family, so...Anyway, Bob, you want to go ahead?"

"Yeah, sure, John," Bob Jogs says. "First of all, Wayne, I am sorry I cannot make it out to your presentation tomorrow afternoon. I had planned to come, but, well, let's just say the duties of department chair can be fickle. I am certain it will go well, though, Wayne, and that everyone – well, the astute anyway - will enjoy it. I have read your whole paper, 'Parking Lot', and it is, indeed, as John likes to say, beguiling." Doc Holiday looks at Floyd and smiles. "There's something about it, too...the voice maybe, or the style, that's hauntingly familiar...I can't quite put my finger on it. Maybe it's the ghost of Socrates, I don't know." Bob Jogs laughs. "Anyway, I'd like to expand on the subject of the paper for a minute, if you all can indulge me?"

"Yes, of course. Please, Bob," Doc Holiday says, "go right ahead."

"Great, thanks. Okay, now, a dictionary's definitions are ultimately just supplemental reports on how words are used in a particular community at a particular time; the only truth value they have is whether or not the people in the community in question actually used the term in the way the dictionary reports; and any correspondence with metaphysical truth, about the way things really are, is merely incidental, and topical. So, treating a dictionary's definitions as true premises for arguments and treating a dictionary's definitions as consistent with one another, as you do, Wayne, ultimately amounts to *mistreatment* of dictionary definitions. But it is a very interesting and instructive, if also maddening, mistreatment.

"What I think it amounts to, in the end, is a big game of 'What if?' You ask the question, What if this dictionary's definitions were not just lexical definitions, or provisional reports of words' usage, but *real* definitions, essential descriptions, of the things in the world the words refer to? What if these definitions described the way things in the world *really* are? Then what? And it's subtle in your paper, Wayne, because you don't come right out and say it, you just enact it, but your answer, it seems to me, is we would find ourselves in an absurd world, and you arrive at that answer, appropriately enough, by a form of argument called reductio ad absurdum, a reduction to the absurd. So you're saying, Look it, if we treat dictionary definitions this way, there are absurd consequences – here they are – therefore we shouldn't treat dictionary definitions in this way. It's a very complex and effective way of arguing, Wayne, and, reading your paper, I'm not sure just how conscious you are of it. Are you aware that reductio is your method of argument here, Wayne?"

"No, well, yes, no, no sir," Floyd says. "It just comes naturally to me."

"Right, right, well. It's all very strange, a very strange game indeed; but I dare say, it is a game not without real, practical application and merit. Like arguments that debunk the Bible, yours exposes the folk myth, under whose influence we have all fallen prey at one time or another, that a dictionary is some sort of absolute, unqualified authority on meanings, words, and the things they refer to. It exposes the way everyone tacitly mistreats a dictionary, it exposes the way everyone erroneously assumes that a dictionary is internally consistent and full, not of provisional definitions of words, but of real definitions of things themselves.

"There's a Socratic aspect, too, Wayne. When Socrates asks someone to tell him what some thing is, when he asks Meno, for example, what virtue is, Meno thinks he has in his mind a real definition, an essential description of the thing in question; however, by the end of the session, we come to find out what Meno has in mind is only the definition of the *word* virtue, not of the *thing* virtue, and that he doesn't *really* know what the definition of the thing virtue is at all. An analogous situation is presented in your paper, Wayne: you set up dictionary definitions to act like real definitions of things, but they come off looking ridiculous, and thus they are exposed as merely lexical definitions of words. So both you and Socrates argue by reductio, yes...

"But a big difference, a big difference is that Socrates always leaves his definitions broken and in pieces; he deconstructs them and leaves them that way. Oddly, Wayne, you, pursuant to not entirely unreasonable methods of definitional substitution and linguistic transitivity – that is, you know, if A equals B and B equals C, then A equals C type stuff - manage to revise and reconstruct your dictionary's definitions somewhere else, as it were, within your dictionary. You play a game in which definitions contained within the universe of your dictionary, are moveable, transitive, and transposable.

"For example, the idea is that either the dictionary definition of parking lot isn't right, that it's faulty, or that there are things in the world we call parking lots that actually aren't worthy of the name parking lot because they do not fit the definition of parking lot. At first you blame the things in the world for being out of compliance with the definition of parking lot, then you turncoat and blame the definition of parking lot for being out of compliance with the things in the world; the definition is too specific. I guess you decide it's easier to change the definition than the world, right? So you take the definition totally apart. Then you put it back together so it's broader, so it better encompasses all the different things in the world we call parking lots; but - and here's the puzzle - when you put it back together, when you reconstruct the definition, you do so by substituting what appear to be equivalent or synonymous terms for the ones you deem problematic. Hence, a paradox: if the substitutions are truly synonymous, following the rule of transitivity, the original definition is synonymous with the reconstructed definition, so what the heck's the difference? What does it all mean, John?" Bob Jogs laughs. Doc Holiday laughs.

"In any case," Bob Jogs says. "That's it; that's where I get off; that's where I extricate myself from the thrall of this neurotic exercise and say to you, Congratulations, Wayne. You have been accepted to Rice University. I got word this morning that a spot has opened up for you in this year's frosh class. So, pack your bags, buddy. Your plane leaves Midland/Odessa at ten o'clock Sunday morning. We're excited to have you on board, Wayne."

"Congratulations, Wayne," Doc Holiday says.

"Fabulous, just fabulous," Nurse Oakley says. "What a big day."

"But Wayne?" Bob Jogs says. "You *are* going to be a

philosophy major now aren't you?"

Everyone laughs. Wayne types.

"Ha ha ha ha of course I'll be a philosophy major that's the whole oh my god I'm so excited oh yes yes thank you Professor Jogs thank you yes."

54

Floyd's asleep. I'm watching the clock on my bedside table. The red numbers say eleven fifty-nine. The numbers change to twelve, there's a light knock on the door, I get out of bed and open the door, I don't see anyone, a hand grabs my leg, I go down to my knees, the hand lets go.

"Shh," Jolly whispers, but I still can't see him, he turns on a small flashlight and shines it into his palm, he's wearing all black, he has on a black hat and black sunglasses and his face and teeth are painted black, he pulls me out into the hall and takes the door to my room and closes it. "Listen. No talking unless it's absolutely necessary. Follow me."

Jolly gets down on his stomach and starts to crawl, he looks back at me and turns off the light, I get down on my stomach, he crawls, I crawl behind him, he crawls about ten feet, he reaches the wall and stops, he sits up and turns on the light into his palm, I sit up. The dumbwaiter is in the wall next to the emergency stairs.

"Stay here," Jolly says. "When I'm inside, close the door then lie down. Lie down on the floor. If somebody comes, pretend to be asleep. They'll think you've been sleepwalking. When I come back, I'll tap the door lightly. You open the door. If you don't open it, I'll know something's wrong and stay inside until you come and get me, whenever the coast is clear. Say 'okay'."

"Okay."

Jolly finds the dumbwaiter door and turns off the light. He pushes the door up. He turns around backwards, puts his arms up into the dumbwaiter shaft and pulls himself up into it. He's gone. I close the door.

I lie down on the floor.

For a long time everything is quiet.

Jolly taps on the dumbwaiter door, I stand up, I open it, he comes out of the shaft and closes the dumbwaiter door, he steps over to the door to the emergency stairs and turns the handle, it opens, we go down the stairs in the dark, Jolly stops at the bottom, turns his light on into his palm and hands it to me, I take it and shine it into my palm, he takes a small black bag off his back and opens it near the light, he takes something out, it's balero it's balero, Jolly takes the light from me and gives me the balero, I reach into my pocket and take out Maria's balero, Jolly pulls the light off of his palm and I compare the two baleros, they are the same.

I put Maria's balero in my left pocket, I put Pablo's balero in my right pocket. Jolly finds the door handle and turns off his light, he opens the door, he looks back at me and points left, I follow him out and close the door onto a piece of wood.

Jolly walks along the edge of The Big House, he runs into the trees, I follow him, under the trees next to Rudy Dude's house, we get behind Rudy Dude's house, Jolly stops and kneels.

"All right, we'll go to the back door. You got the balero?" I take Pablo's balero out of my right pocket. "Okay. Let's go."

We go up to the back door, we stand there, Jolly points to the doorbell, I put my finger near it, he pokes his finger forward, I push the bell, the bell goes "ding-dong."

We wait.

Jolly taps me and pokes his finger forward, I put my finger near the bell, he pokes his finger forward, I push the bell, "Ding dong."

We wait.

There are sounds inside the house, someone's coming, I hold up Pablo's balero.

"Goddammit," Rudy Dude says through the door. "This better be good." He opens the door. "Holy shit!" He steps back into his house, he's wearing pajamas and a robe. "What...what the fuck are you two idiots doing? Jolly, take off those fucking sunglasses." Jolly takes off the sunglasses. "And what the fuck is that Birdsong? Ball-in-a-cup? You sneak down here in the middle of the goddamn night and wake me up to play fucking ball-in-a-cup? What the...Put it down, Birdsong. Get that goddamn thing out of my face, and somebody tell me what the hell's going on around here."

"No, no, Mr. Dude. See?" I say. "It's Pablo's balero, it's Pablo's balero."

"Pablo's ba...Pablo's balero? What the fuck are you talking about, Pablo's balero, Birdsong?"

"Here, see?" I hand Pablo's balero to him but he doesn't take it. "It's, it's Pablo's balero. Jolly found it in the warden's house tonight." Rudy Dude opens his eyes wide. "It's the same as Maria's balero." I reach into my left pocket, I take out Maria's balero and hold it up too. "See, Mr. Dude? They're the same, they're the same, they're..."

"Whoa." Rudy Dude points at me. "Stop right there, Birdsong. Stop right there." I lower the baleros. "Did I just hear you say Jolly found that thing *in the warden's house tonight*?"

"Yes, yes."

"So he...Jolly, you were *inside* the warden's house tonight?"

"Yes, sir. I penetrated the interior, obtained the object, and went undetected, sir."

"You mean you broke into her house and took that thing?"

"Well...yes, no. No sir. Not exactly, sir. I'm going to put it back, sir."

"Holy shit," Rudy Dude steps aside and opens the door. "Get in here. Get the fuck in here, goddamnit." Jolly and I go in. "Jesus shit. Living room," Rudy Dude points behind him. "Go. Sit."

Jolly and I go in the living room and sit on the couch. "You said he was going to be happy, man," Jolly says.

There's a big fireplace, and there are animal heads on all the walls, there's a bear and a moose and a mountain lion and a javelina and a boar and a duck and a fish, Rudy Dude closes the backdoor.

Rudy Dude comes in and sits in a big brown chair across from us, he shakes his head. "Why? What in god's name possessed you to do something as stupid as that? Goddammit. You idiots don't know what you're dealing with here; you don't know what you're doing; you run amok; you fuck things up." He looks at the floor. "It was them fucking Mexicans." He looks up at us. "They got to you. They recruited you. Had to be. But hey, you tell me. Enlighten me. Now, dip-shits."

"Come on, Birdsong," Jolly whispers.

"Birdsong?" Rudy Dude says. "Come on, son. I ain't got all night."

I look into the carpet.

"All right, Jolly. He can't do it. It's too much for him..."

"No! I can do it," I say to the floor, Maria is singing. "I can do it...Maria. Maria, at the dance, she said...'Harris, I have to talk to you, Harris. I have to ask you somethings. Es muy importante. I sorry. I try to speak English. Harris. I in trouble because my brother. I lose him. Now he is gone, and it's all my fault. My brother, his name is Pablo. He is ten years old. He just a little boy'."

"Wait a minute, wait a minute, Birdsong," Rudy Dude says. "What the hell are you doing, son? What the hell is he doing, Jolly? He's fucking possessed. I won't have none of this Mexican hoodoo shit in my house, Jolly."

"No, no sir. He's just got everything Maria said to him memorized exactly. That's how he does it. That's how he's going to tell you, sir. Please, let him go on, sir."

"Jesus shit, y'all are pushing me, Jolly. Y'all are pushing me way out past what I can tolerate here."

Jolly puts his hand on my back. "Go ahead, Birdsong. You got it."

I say the song that Maria sings...

"'...Harris, if you no do this, the warden, she know, she know somebody been in her house, and she going to kill Pablo, Harris,'" I say, I sit up.

"Whoa. Holy shit," Rudy Dude says. "You done?"

"Yes, yes, I'm done."

"You're free, from the...spell or whatever it was?"

"Yes."

"And you're okay?"

"Yes, I'm okay."

"Wow, Birdsong. I got to tell you, that was...that was very uncomfortable for me. That concerned me. You appeared to be possessed, like that Maria had complete control over you and what you were saying, like she had shut down your body and was talking through you." He stares at me. "But there's no way. So, I got to ask, what was really happening there, Birdsong?"

"I, I was listening to Maria sing, Mr. Dude. Everything Maria said to me at the dance is a song. That's how I remember."

"Mm. Well, however you do it...I mean, I knew you'd memorized a dictionary, which is..." He shakes his head. "Anyway, goddamnit, look it." He points at us. "Both of you. This is serious, serious business we're dealing with here, and what y'all done is a fuck-up, a big fucking fuck-up, okay; I don't care how innocent or beneficent your intentions were. By breaking into the warden's house and taking that fucking...ball-in-a-cup, and then coming down here, y'all not only committed a felony, for which you could spend good time in prison, you also implicated me in that felony, and you put into jeopardy all the proper legal actions which my attorney and I have been pursuing concerning the removal of my sister as warden of this ranch. This is America, goddammit, not Mexico. We don't take matters into our own hands just because we're inspired by some fucking...vision, some fantastical story drummed up out of our imaginations; we follow the rules of evidence, we follow dictates of the logic of the law.

"Birdsong, Maria is a fifteen year-old Mexican girl from a little family of wetbacks. Everything's all...mythological with them. You've been recruited, Birdsong, recruited to do the handiwork of a people motivated by superstition. You come down here all swinging dicks with that fucking ball-in-a-cup, but..." Rudy Dude reaches his hand toward me. "Here, let me see that piece of shit."

I stand up and hand Pablo's balero to Rudy Dude. He looks at it. He tries to get the ball in the cup. He tries again. He tries again. "Fuck," he says. He tries again. He gets the ball in the cup. "Okay. But this ain't no Holy Grail; this ain't the Holy Grail you think it is, Birdsong. They got these by the dozen down at Bill's Dollar in Ft. Davis, and they all look exactly like this. Everybody's got one just like this one. Ain't nothing special about it looking the same as Maria's." He looks carefully at Pablo's balero. "Ain't no identifying marks on it that say, 'Pablo's balero'." He hands Pablo's balero out to me. I get up and get it and sit back down. I hold the two baleros and look at them. "Can you imagine me going to the sheriff and saying, 'Hey Chuck, listen, two of my boys at the ranch broke into the warden's house and took this ball-in-a-cup. The Mexicans at the ranch have been bending their ears, and they say it belongs to a little Mexican boy named Pablo and that the warden's got Pablo locked up in a cage inside in her house. I figure that's good enough for probable cause and Judge Eckel's signature on the search warrant, don't you?" Rudy Dude laughs. He stops laughing.

"Look, guys, Judy might've gone nuts, but I'm sorry, there ain't no Mexican boy locked up in a cage in her house playing ball-in-a-cup. He's been eaten up by javelinas or mountain lions, just like Geener. Or one of his perverted uncle's buried him, god forbid..."

"But, who, who is Preston, Mr. Dude?" I say.

"Preston? Oh, no Birdsong, no, no. Preston is not a Mexican...unless he's a Chihuahua." Rudy Dude laughs.

"But, tia Rosalía said..."

"Look, Birdsong. Listen to me. Tia Rosalía might be a liar; Maria might be a liar. They might've lied to you to get you to do what they want. And even if they're telling the truth, Birdsong, Judy could've gotten any manner of pet between Rosalía's last day and today. Obviously. Also, the penthouse is a big place, much bigger than you think. Judy may have never permitted Rosalía to go beyond a certain point. There's even a garden up there, an outdoor garden with grass and plants. Did you know that? Maybe that's where...Well shit, Jolly, you were just up there. Did you see any evidence of a pet? You must have been worried there might be a dog."

"Yes sir, I was aware of the possibility that there might be a dog, sir, but I am always prepared for anything and everything, sir." Jolly takes hold of his black utility belt with both hands. "I got everything from dog treats to poison darts in here. But no, no sir. I searched a limited area too, sir, but I didn't see any pet stuff up there. Well, unless you count a picture. I did see a picture of the warden with a big snake around her neck."

"See, Birdsong? There you go."

"But sir?" Jolly says. "I was wondering about what Maria said about putting the balero back, sir? Should I go back up into the warden's and put it back where I found it?"

"What? Jolly! Hell no! And risk getting caught again? No. Fuck no, buddy, come on."

"But," I say, "if, if she sees that it's gone, she she's..."

"Birdsong, dammit," Rudy Dude says. "How many times do I have to tell you? Pablo is not in the warden's house and the warden will never miss the ball-in-a-cup. Christ, even if she did, she'd never think someone broke in and stole it; she'd just think she misplaced it. Where, where was it in her house, Jolly? Where, exactly, did you find it?"

"It was on a shelf, with some books and other things."

"Right, never miss it."

"What, what do I tell Maria?" I say.

Rudy Dude looks into the fireplace. "Yeah, all right, Birdsong, all right." He looks at me. "Here, tell her this. Memorize and tell her exactly this and only this. No more, you hear me?"

"Yes, yes."

"All right, you say: 'The ball-in-a-cup game is not necessarily Pablo's; everyone around here has one just like it; it does not prove Pablo is inside the warden's house, and even if it did, it couldn't be used as evidence because it was illegally obtained. Please be patient, remain calm, and rest assured that the ranch is making every effort to determine what happened to Pablo'. That should do it. I'm sure I'll have to answer to them, as well, so...yeah. Soon enough, they're going to know Pablo is not and never was in the warden's house."

"But, but why did that boy in the warden's story get killed by Delia the mayor?"

Rudy Dude stands up. "Look, Birdsong. That story was just that, a story, fiction. Judy just made it up to scare everybody into leaving her alone, okay? Come on. Live in reality, son. Now everybody up. Let's go. That's all the hoodoo I can stand for one night. Get back to your rooms."

Jolly and I stand up. Rudy Dude stops us and puts his hands on our shoulders.

"And hey. Consider yourselves lucky. Under normal circumstances, I would not only have to make up a ranch behavior violation report, but, because your transgression was so severe, because it was fucking criminal, guys, I'd have to report you - not the warden - *you* to the sheriff. You hear me? But these are not normal circumstances, and I can't do either because, well, for one, y'all did mean well;

you're idiots, but you did mean well; you were trying to help me, and other people, and I don't want to see you go to jail for that. Also, making those reports would jeopardize the legal cases my attorney and I have building against Judy right now. They'd cause us to have to change our focus, and they'd tip Judy off. If she thought people were sneaking around her house looking for shit, she'd blame me, clean up her act, and start building her case against *me*, you understand? She'd accuse me of being complicit with you all, and it'd be all over.

"So listen. Except for what I told you to tell Maria, not a word to anybody about any about this, okay? *Not a single fucking word*, you hear me?" Jolly and I say okay. "Right. Now get the fuck out of here."

Rudy Dude walks us to the door. He opens it. We walk out.

"Oh, and Birdsong. I noticed you finished moving that mountain of rocks. That's good work. Good work, son." Rudy Dude closes the door.

Jolly puts on his sunglasses. We run into the trees. I stop Jolly before we get to the edge of the The Big House.

"Jolly, Jolly," I whisper. "Please, please put the balero back in the warden's house, Jolly. I promised Maria. I promised her, Jolly."

"What? Rudy said no way, man. So no, no way."

"Jolly, I promised Maria. I assured her that it will certainly happen or be done. I assured her..."

"No."

"Jolly, if, if you don't do it, then I'm going to, I'm going to do it; I'm going to put the balero back in the warden's house."

"What? Are you serious?"

"Yes, yes, Jolly. I'm serious. If you don't put it back, then I am going to put it back."

"Oh, fucking shit, Birdsong. Shit. All right, all right, give me that thing."

I give him Pablo's balero. He puts it into his backpack.

We go into The Big House and up the stairs to the infirmary.

Jolly opens the dumbwaiter door and climbs in. He closes the dumbwaiter door. I lie down on the floor. Everything is quiet.

Jolly knocks on the dumbwaiter door, I stand up and open the door, he slips out of the shaft and onto the floor, he puts his mouth close to my ear and whispers, "The dumbwaiter is up." I step back he steps forward he hands me Pablo's balero. "Bye-bye," he says he opens the door to the emergency stairs and disappears I stand there.

I go into my room I get undressed I get in bed.

Floyd types. "Harris, what are you doing."

I sit up.

"Harris."

I walk over to Floyd lying in his chair I stand over him.

"Just what do you think you're doing, Harris."

I reach behind his chair he starts to bring it upright.

"I really think I'm entitled to an answer to that question, Harris."

I feel behind the speaker.

"Look Harris, I can see you're really upset. Harris, stop. Will you stop, Harris. Stop Harris..."

"Shut the fuck up, Floyd," I say I pull the wire out of the back of the speaker.

55

Nurse Oakley knocks on the door, I wake up, I open my eyes, Floyd hits his fingers on his keyboards, but he doesn't say anything and he doesn't go anywhere.

"Yoo hoo," Nurse Oakley says through the door. "Anybody home?" She cracks the door. "May I come in?" She pushes the door open. "Morning." She comes in. She's carrying The Book. "Harris, hey, sleepyhead. What are you doing still in bed?"

Floyd hits his fingers on his keyboards.

"Morning, Wayne. What's wrong with your..." Nurse Oakley sets down The Book on Floyd's desk next to his computer screen. She goes over and touches Floyd's keyboards. She taps a few keys. She leans over and inspects them. "Hm. Definitely not my specialty. Harris, you know anything about this? Harris? Harris, come on, sweetheart, time to get up."

Nurse Oakley goes around behind Floyd's chair. She kneels and pulls the recharge cable out of the wall. The cable recoils inside the back of the chair. "Now, maybe if I..." She flips the switch on the back of the chair from recharge to drive, Floyd lurches forward into the center of the room. "Whoa!" she says and stands up, Floyd makes two circles in the middle of the room and rams my bed, he backs up and rams my bed again. "Wayne, for Pete's sake! Stop!" Nurse

Oakley says, Floyd rams my bed again. "Harris, get up!" I get out of bed on the other side, Floyd rounds the end of my bed, I run past the window and into the bathroom, I shut the door, Floyd rams the door. "Wayne! Stop that! Right now, dammit!"

Everything's quiet. I crack the door. They're over at Floyd's desk.

Floyd stretches his hand for the cable lying on his desk. It connects his keyboards to the computer. "What? This?" Nurse Oakley says and picks up the cable. Floyd sticks up his thumb. He points to the side of his right keyboard. "In here? Ah, I see." She plugs the cable into his keyboard. Floyd types. Nurse Oakley looks at the computer screen. She looks behind the speaker on Floyd's chair. Floyd's tapping his keyboards. She plugs the speaker wire into the back of the speaker.

"Plbrtstafubblesttt...motherfucker," Floyd says.

"Wayne, language," Nurse Oakley says.

"Harris did it he unplugged my speaker last night he was out sneaking around and I asked him what he was doing and he told me to shut the he told me to shut up and unplugged my speaker what if I had an emergency in the middle of the night and needed help..."

"Wayne, Wayne, slow down, honey. Slow down."

"He did it Harris did it."

Nurse Oakley looks toward the bathroom. "Harris. Harris, come on out of there now. Harris."

I open the door and stand in the doorway.

"Is this true, Harris. Did you unplug Wayne's speaker last night?"

"Yes."

"Why, Harris? Why did you do that?"

"He, he was bothering me. He was talking in his sleep. He's always talking in his sleep and bothering me."

"Harris, that is a serious no-no. It is absolutely imperative that Wayne be able to communicate at all times if he needs to. There's a way for you to control the volume, or turn it down at night, isn't there, Wayne?"

"Yes, I always turn the volume down at night."

"No, no he doesn't. He doesn't always turn it down at night."

"That's bullshit. I always turn it down."

"Wayne, please," Nurse Oakley says. "All right, look guys, you've only got one more night together, right?"

"Two. Two more," Floyd says. "Tonight, camping, and tomorrow night back here, after the rodeo. I leave on Sunday morning."

"Okay, two nights then. That's all you've got. Surely you can manage that without tampering with Floyd's speaker again, Harris, okay?"

"Okay."

"Ask him what he was doing sneaking around in the middle of the night," Floyd says. "What were you doing going in and out of the room last night, Harris. There was someone else here too, wasn't there."

"Harris?" Nurse Oakley says.

"I wasn't sneaking around; I was sleepwalking. I woke up in the hallway and came back in."

"Sleepwalking. Wayne was sleeptalking, and you were sleepwalking. Really, Harris?"

"Yes, yes. First, I was sleepwalking. I woke up in the hall and came back in. Then Floyd was sleeptalking."

"I wasn't sleeptalking," Floyd says. "I was asking him what he thought he was doing sneaking in and out of the room."

"Well, okay Wayne, I hear you, but I guess if Harris says he was sleepwalking, and there's no other evidence to the contrary, then..."

"No. I heard someone else at the door. There was someone else here, Nurse Oakley."

"Okay. Harris, tell the truth. Was there anyone else here last night? Did you have a visitor?"

"No."

"He's lying. You're a liar, Harris."

"Wayne, that's enough. Yes, that is all together enough. Let's just put all this behind us now, shall we?" Nurse Oakley looks at her watch. "Oh, it's late. Wayne, you're due down at Doc Holiday's in half an hour to work on your presentation. So come on, Harris, let's get him showered and dressed. Then you and I will have our last powwow of the term. You have a journal entry ready for me, I assume?"

"No. I forgot. I forgot we were going to meet for class today."

"Harris, that's not like you."

"He was too busy sneaking around."

"I thought the Mexican Fiesta yesterday, in Doc Holiday's office, was the end."

"All right, well, after Wayne, you get showered then take a minute and write a quick journal entry for me, for yesterday, okay? And remember: thought, emotion, composition."

56

Wayne and Nurse Oakley leave. I take a shower and put on my regular clothes. I open the bedroom door. The hall's empty. The dumbwaiter doors are closed. I close the door and go to the window. I get my journal out of my closet and go over to Floyd's desk and sit down. I take a pen out of the drawer and open my journal. I write "August 15" at the top of the page.

I put the pen inside my journal and close it. I stand up, take my journal and The Book in one hand, grab the back of the chair with the other, and go over to the window. I set the chair down across from the armchair and put my journal and The Book down on the seat of the armchair. I go to the bedside table. I pick up the phone and call Nurse Oakley. I go back and sit down in the chair and look out the window.

57

Nurse Oakley puts on her glasses and opens my journal. She takes out the pen. She turns the page. She closes my journal and takes off her glasses.

"Okay, Harris." She smiles. "We'll give you a pass today. You have done an incredible job. Your sentence structure, your grammar and punctuation have gone from non-existent to perfect, impeccable, in no time at all." She shakes her head. "I suppose it's obvious to you now how these things help us to slow down and organize our thoughts; they should be especially helpful in dealing with complex logical deductions like the ones you deal with frequently, Harris...Harris, haven't you found these things helpful?"

"Yes."

"Harris, is there something going on outside I should know about?"

"No, ma'am."

"Are you sure? Because you seem distracted, honey. Are you upset about something?"

"No."

"Okay, but you know you can talk to me about anything in complete confidence?"

"Yes."

"Harris, let me ask you: how do you feel about the other ranch hands, especially Wayne, getting to leave the ranch on

Sunday when you have to stay here?"

"I dislike it."

"Why's that, Harris? Does that make you sad?"

"If to dislike something is to be upset, if to be upset is to be in pain, and if to be in pain is to be sad; then, I am sad."

"Does it make you angry?"

"If to dislike something is to be upset, if to be upset is to be in pain, and to be in pain is to be angry; then, I am angry."

"Okay. Harris. I want to know how *you really feel*, not how dictionary definitions and logic say you *should* feel. How do *you really feel*, Harris?"

"I dislike it."

"Right, I know, Harris, but I'm trying to go deeper with you here. So, I guess what I really want to know is, Are you in pain?"

"I already told you, Nurse Oakley. If to dislike something is to be upset, and if to be upset is to be in pain; then, yes, I am in pain."

58

The phone rings, I open my eyes, I pick it up.

"Harris? Harris, you there?" It's Nurse Oakley.

"Yes."

"Come on down, honey. Your buddies, Mr. Wau and Mr. Jolly are here. Harris?"

"Yes."

"Oh goodness, it's almost three. Time to head over to the auditorium for Wayne's presentation."

I get out of bed and go down the hall.

Nurse Oakley looks up from her computer. "You all go ahead." She looks back down. "I'll be along; I've just got to wrap this...darn it," she says to the screen.

Me and Cosmic and Jolly get in the elevator. The doors close.

"So," Jolly says. "Everything cool?"

I look at Cosmic.

"He knows, Birdsong. He knows all about it. I had to have an alibi. What'd you think? I was going do all that shit last night without an alibi?" He points to his head. "All right, so come on, man. Everything's cool, right?"

"I don't know."

"Well, nothing happened last night after I left, or this morning, that I should know about, did it?"

"No."

"Then everything's cool." The doors open. We walk out of The Big House and go down the steps. Jolly stops me at the bottom. "Birdsong, don't worry. If something was going to blow up, it would have done it by now, okay? We're in the clear. Trust me. I'm a fucking professional, man."

Cosmic laughs. "Then what are you doing *here*, dude?"

"Shut the fuck up, Cosmic. Listen. I'm sure the warden has no idea I was up in there last night, and I'm sure she'll never notice that fucking ball-in-a-cup is missing, okay? That dumbwaiter shit was pure coincidence. Man, she can get up and use that thing whenever she wants, and she just happened to use it the middle of the night last night. Shit, maybe that's when she always uses it, in the middle of the night. The main thing is, the *lucky* thing is we didn't cross paths...that would've sucked...but we didn't, man; we didn't, so it's fucking all good. And Birdsong. Look it. I thought, *maybe*, at first too, bro, but..." He shakes his head. "...Rudy's right: there ain't no Mexican boy up there. I mean, that's nuts, Birdsong, you know? That's nuts."

"Uh oh," Cosmic says.

"What?" Jolly says.

There's someone standing on the other side of the road it's Maria she's wearing a long white apron that goes behind her neck and down to her knees it has red and brown stains all over it she walks around the dining hall toward the back toward the kitchen.

"No," Jolly says. "There's no 'Uh oh', Cosmic. Birdsong, it's fine, man. Just go over there and tell her exactly what Rudy Dude told you to tell her. That's all you got to do. So go. Go ahead, man. It's all good. We'll see you in the auditorium."

We cross the road, Cosmic and Jolly go toward the

auditorium, I walk around the dining hall toward the back, toward the kitchen, there is a whistle, Maria is standing in a corner outside between the dining hall and the kitchen, I walk up to her and stop.

"Oh, Dios mio, Harris! Que pasó? Tia Rosalía, she tell me, the dumbwaiter, it is up, this morning it is up," Maria takes my hands. "Please tell me, everything is okay?"

"I, I don't know, Maria."

"Why you don't know? Why you don't know, Harris? I see Jolly, he is out from the warden house."

"Yes."

"Si, bueno. So...he get something of Pablo, Harris? Pablo balero?"

"Yes, he, he got...a balero, Maria, but..."

"Ay dios mio, Harris. Dios mio, dios mio." She squeezes my hands. "And you, you show it to Rudy Dude, Harris?"

"Yes, yes."

"Well, what he say, Harris? He will help us now, Harris? He call the sheriff now?"

I shake my head.

"No! No, Harris! You no shake your head. You no shake your head. You tell me good news, Harris. You tell me. What he say, Harris?"

"He said..."

"Harris, dime todo."

"He said, 'The ball-in-a-cup game is not necessarily Pablo's...'"

"Not...not Pablo balero? It is the same as my balero, Harris?"

"Yes."

"And you show him both balero, Harris?"

"Yes."

"Then he see, Harris. He see it's Pablo balero, Harris. Harris."

"He said, 'Everyone around here has one just like it; it does not prove Pablo is inside the warden's house, and even if it did, it couldn't be used as evidence because it was illegally obtained...'"

"Oh, no, no, no, no, no, Harris. No! Rudy Dude, he see Pablo balero. He help us now! He call the sheriff now!"

"No, no. Rudy Dude said, 'Please be patient, remain calm, and rest assured that the ranch is making every effort to determine what happened to Pablo'."

Maria drops her head. "Ay dios mio, dios mio, no comprendo. No es verdad." Her tears fall on my hands. "Es un mentiroso."

She looks up at me, her face is red and wet. "But Harris," she says, she smiles. "Still, everything, it is okay, no? Be...because Jolly, he put back Pablo balero, inside the warden house before she...before the dumbwaiter, she bring it up, Harris."

I pull my hands out of hers, I put them into my pockets and pull out the two baleros, I put them into her hands, she takes them but she does not look at them, tears pour out of her eyes, she says, "Esto...esto será el fin de todo. This will be the end of everything."

59

I open the door and step inside the auditorium. Floyd's voice is coming over the speaker system. It's dark, but he's sitting in the light, in the spotlight, on the stage. There's a microphone stand on one side of him holding a microphone up to the speaker on his chair. Doc Holiday is standing on the other side of him with his arm on a music stand. He turns a page of paper. A lot of the seats in the auditorium are filled. I go down the aisle. Someone grabs my shirt and pulls. I sit down.

"Where the hell you been?" Jolly whispers. "You weren't out there talking the whole time were you?"

"No, no."

"You only said what you were supposed to say, nothing more, right?"

"Yes, yes."

"Well then what the fuck took you so long?"

The person in front of us turns around and says, "Shh." It's a student, a young girl.

"I went to the storage shed for a while. My stomach hurt."

"Hey, you can't let shit get to you like this, Birdsong. You got to stay strong, bro. Everything's going to be fine."

The girl turns around again. "Please," she says.

"...So, recall," Floyd says, "our original question: If an

automobile is a vehicle designed to carry a small number of passengers, and a passenger is somebody who travels in a vehicle but is not a driver; then, who's going to drive the automobile? If you have been following the argument I have been tracing through The Book, this dictionary, then you already know the answer, but in case you missed it, here it is in full:

"If a driver provides motivation, to provide is to be the source of something, and motivation is the cognitive force that activates and directs behavior, then a driver is the source of the cognitive force that activates and directs behavior, and if cognitive relates to thought, then a driver is the source of thought that activates and directs behavior; but, if thought is the activity of thinking and thinking is the use of the mind to form thought in general, then the mind is the source of thought in general and a driver is an aspect of the mind that is the source of thought that activates and directs behavior in particular; if a passenger is somebody who travels in a motor vehicle but is not a driver, then a passenger is somebody who travels in a motor vehicle but is not the area of the mind that is the source of thought that activates behavior, and if somebody is a person and a person is a human being's body, then a passenger is a body who travels in a motor vehicle but is not the area of the mind that is the source of thought that activates behavior; but, if a body is the complete material structure of a human being, material relates to or consists of solid physical matter, and matter is something that is extended in space and persists through time and is contrasted with mind, then a body is something that is extended in space and persists through time and is contrasted with mind and a passenger is something that is extended in space and persists through time and is contrasted with mind who travels in a motor vehicle and is not the area of the mind that is the source of thought that activates behavior; now, if a duality is a situation or nature that has two parts that are complementary or opposed to each other and mind and body form a situation or nature that has two parts that are complementary or opposed to each other, then mind and body form a duality, and if a passenger is a body and a driver is an aspect of the mind, then passenger and driver form a duality and passenger and driver are complementary or opposed; if passenger and driver are complementary, then they make a pair or whole; if passenger and driver make a pair and a pair is to be regarded as two objects, then passenger and driver are to be regarded as two objects; if passenger and driver are to be regarded as two objects and passenger and driver are opposed, then a passenger is somebody who travels in a motor vehicle but is not a driver; if passenger and driver make a whole and a whole is something regarded as a single entity, then passenger and driver are also to be regarded as a single entity; if passenger and driver are to be regarded as a single entity and an automobile is a vehicle designed to carry a small number of passengers, then an automobile is also a vehicle designed to carry a small, equal number of drivers, and if an automobile is designed to carry a small number of drivers, then a driver, acting as the source of the cognitive force that activates and directs the behavior of a concomitant passenger, is driving the automobile. Thank you."

The auditorium is silent. Doc Holiday claps. Some people clap with him. He takes the microphone. "Thank you, Wayne. That was very, very interesting. Okay, now, does any one have any questions? Any questions for Wayne?" He looks around. "Anyone...no...all right, well, if not, then please congratulate Wayne on his paper and his acceptance to Rice. Thanks everybody for coming, and have a great end-of-term weekend." Everyone gets up and files out.

"Well come on, Birdsong, get up. It's over, man. Let's go," Jolly says. "Time to go camping."

60

"We'll put your guys' tent up here, in number six," Jolly says. "It's bigger." He drops Floyd's and my tent bag, walks over to the next campsite, and drops the other tent bag. "We'll put ours up here, in number seven. Rudy did say use six and seven, right?"

The campsites are in the trees across the road from the big field. The land behind the campsites slopes up a little and becomes the mountains farther on. There are trails all around.

"Yes, six and seven," Floyd says.

"Cool," Jolly takes off his backpack. Cosmic and I take off our backpacks. "Birdsong, you can sleep in our tent, if you want. Yours doesn't have a floor on it, you know...for Floyd, but he...you said you sleep up off the ground, in your chair, didn't you, Floyd?"

"Yes."

"Yeah, so he's going to be up out of the way of scorpions and shit, but you, you'd be in your sleeping bag, but you'd just be on lying on the ground, so..."

"I want to sleep in your tent," I say.

"Yes, that's good, he can sleep in your tent," Floyd says.

"Cool." Jolly put his fists on his hips and looks at the fire pit. "Nice. Big pile of firewood, already collected and ready to burn." He nods his head. "All right, well. Let's get these tents up. Cosmic, you set up number seven. Me and Birdsong'll get number six."

Jolly comes back over to number six and kneels down next to the tent bag. "This one's going to be like a big living room," he says and unzips the bag. He dumps the tent out on the ground.

I walk into the campsite. The ground is soft. I press it with the toe of my boot.

"Remember clearing all these sites last year, Cosmic?" Jolly says.

"Like, no, dude," Cosmic says. "I don't want to remember that."

Jolly laughs. "Here, Birdsong, you start setting up the frame." He pushes the frame aside. "I'll get the tent part all situated."

I carry the frame out of the campsite and start unfolding it. Jolly spreads the big blue tent flat over the ground then drags it off to one side. "All right, frame," he says. He comes over and takes the frame from me. Jolly opens the frame halfway and sets it in the middle of the campsite. He looks over at Cosmic. "How's it coming over there, man?"

"It's, it's all stuck together, dude. How do you get these poles out?"

"Man, it's the same one as last year, remember? You don't get the poles out. It's all inter-connected. It's easy." Cosmic stands there looking at him. "All right, just put it down, bro. I'll get it in a minute."

Cosmic drops the tent and sits down on a log.

"Birdsong, come over here and help me get the tent over the frame."

Jolly and I take the tent and pull it over the frame. Jolly finds the door. He unzips it, goes inside, and pushes open the frame all the way. The tent expands to full size. It's big and blue. It has four walls and a pointed roof. "All right, that's it," Jolly says from inside. Come on in, check it out."

I go in.

"Well, what do you think? It's nice, right?"

"Yes, yes."

Jolly goes around and unzips the windows and rolls them up. "Hey, Socrates! Get in here and check out your new digs, bro!"

Floyd drives into the tent. "Very nice."

Cosmic comes in. "Whoa ho. It's like a party tent, dudes."

"Yep," Jolly says. "That is exactly what it is, and that is exactly what it's going to be." He holds up a finger. "Wait right here, gentlemen. I'll be right back."

Cosmic and I look out the window. Jolly unzips his backpack. He takes out two brown containers and sets them on the ground. He turns around. "Watch and learn, fellows," he says. He stands up and goes over to the other tent. He walks around it and snaps all the poles into place. He turns to us. "Voila!" The tent is up. He grabs the two bottles.

Jolly comes back into the tent smiling and holding the two brown containers up on either side of his face. One is Jack Daniels Whiskey; the other is a large glass jar filled with thick brown liquid. He looks from one to the other.

"Like, wow, bro," Cosmic says. "Where'd you get that shit? What's in the jar?"

Jolly brings the bottles down and looks at them. "I got that shit from mi amigo, Javier, in Winter Park, Colorado, and what's in the jar is..." He looks at us. "Peyote."

"Peyote," Cosmic whispers.

"Yeah, peyote," Jolly whispers. Cosmic nods.

Floyd types. "Hey, I'm ready. I'm ready to party. I'm

excited."

"You, you don't even know what peyote is, Floyd, and if you don't know what peyote is, then you're ignorant."

"Ha ha ha, Harris. I never claimed to know what peyote is; I only expressed an interest in partying."

"Well, if you're so smart, then what is it, what is peyote, Floyd? See, see, you're ignorant, you lack knowledge, you're unaware of, of something. It's any one of the button-shaped nodules on the stem of the peyote cactus that contains mescaline and is used as a hallucinogenic drug."

"Look, Harris. Just because you memorized a dictionary doesn't mean you know what anything really is," Floyd says. "You've just memorized a bunch of sounds, or songs, or whatever..."

"And, you stole my song too, Floyd. You stole my automobile song and put it in your paper, and if you stole my song, then you are a thief. Now you're an ignorant thief."

"That's just bullshit, Harris."

"Stole your automobile song?" Jolly says.

"He means argument. He's accusing me of stealing his argument."

"Yes, yes, Floyd, if I showed you that argument, then you stole it."

"No, Harris. I asked you questions, and you answered them, then I sorted out the argument. It's my argument."

"But, if, if I hadn't given you the answers, then you wouldn't have an argument."

"No, that's not true, Harris. You forget. I have The Book, that dictionary, now, too, the same as you. I have access to all the same answers and information as you."

"But, but you, you didn't have it then, and you, you don't always know where to look in The Book, Floyd, and if, if you don't always know where to look, then you don't always have the information firmly in mind, and if you don't always have the information firmly in mind, then you don't always have the capacity to reason, and if you don't always have the capacity to reason, then you don't always have the capacity to think logically, and if you don't always have the capacity to think logically, then you don't always have the capacity to think in a way relating to philosophical logic, and if I do, if I always do; then, then I, I am a better philosopher than you, Floyd."

"Cosmic, wow, dude," Cosmic says.

"Harris," Floyd says. "I hate to disappoint you, but what you have proven, through your little...demonstration, is: one, that you are not a philosopher of any sort by any stretch of the imagination; and, two, that what you are, that all you are is a dictionary, a reference book, and not even a very good one at that."

"Shut the fuck up, Floyd! Am too! I am too a philosopher now! You, you don't know! You don't know anything, Floyd!"

"Okay, guys, guys," Jolly says. "That's enough, that's enough. Damn, let's bury this hatchet, for Christ's sake? Jesus. Birdsong, listen. It should make you feel better to know that, before you got to the auditorium this afternoon, when Doc Holiday was introducing Floyd, he mentioned you, and he thanked you for all your help. Didn't you and Doc thank him, Floyd?"

"Yes, yes, that's right. We thanked him."

"Well would it kill you to thank him again now, Floyd?" Jolly says.

"Jolly, this guy, last night this guy..."

"This guy what, Floyd?" Jolly says.

"Oh fuck it. Nothing. It was nothing. Harris, thank you. Thank you for all your help. Your contribution to my project has been invaluable, and I couldn't have done it without you."

"All right, all right. Did you hear that, Birdsong? See?"

I don't say anything.

"Oh, come on. Now look, guys. We're going to have fun tonight if it kills us. And here's what we're going to do. I got it all planned out: we're going to do a community whiskey shot, right now, to get in the spirit; then we're going to go to the barbeque and storyteller thing at the amphitheater; then, on the way back, we're going to stop by the shed and pick up some bows and arrows; then we're going to come back here, stoke up a fire, do a bunch of whiskey shots, and drink all that peyote; then we're going to go on a little hunting expedition, led by yours truly, before it gets too dark, maybe shoot us a javelina or a wild pig or something – Floyd, the trails are good and, with us and those all terrain tires, you won't have any trouble - and then we're going to come back here and sit around the fire and freak out on the flames. Okay? Sound good?"

"Yeah, yeah, sounds good, sounds good," Cosmic and Floyd say.

"Good. Now, what's the best way to get a shot of whiskey into your ass, Floyd?"

I walk across the road into the big field.

"Birdsong. Birdsong!" Jolly says, he's outside the tent. "Where are you going, man? Come on!"

I keep walking.

67

I don't need them, if I don't need them, then they are not essential to me, they're stupid, if they're stupid they show a lack of intelligence or are irritatingly silly or time-wasting, I don't need them because they're stupid. I want to be alone, if I want to be alone, then I want to be without the assistance or company of others, and if I want to be without the assistance of others, then I want to be without help, and if I want to be without the company of others, then I want to have no people to associate with.

I pass the shed and the archery targets and go around the hill behind Rudy Dude's house. Rudy Dude's truck is parked behind his house. I walk past the truck. There are two dirt roads: one leads straight away from the ranch over an open field toward the highway; the other comes from the front part of the ranch, runs around the side of The Big House, crosses the first road behind Rudy Dude's, and turns into a trail that runs into the trees and hills to my right. There are some balloons and a sign in the trees. I walk to the sign. The sign is a wooden arrow. It says, "Amphitheater - 0.5". It points down the trail.

I walk down the trail. It goes up a little, and around, in and under the trees, there's laughing, I stop.

I go on. There's a scream and more laughing, there's movement ahead through the trees, people, children, I stop, turn around, voices, children's, a woman's, are coming from behind me, they're coming up the trail behind me talking, laughing children and a woman are coming up the trail, they're in front of me, they're behind me, she's coming, I duck into the trees and run as fast as I can I break branches with my arms and body I run deep into the woods away from the trail, I reach the steep side of a mountain and run along it, I drop down to the ground behind a boulder and wait.

I wait. There's nothing. I stand on my knees and lean around the boulder, there's no one, no one, nothing, nothing but trees and everything is quiet, except my breathing. I catch my breath. Everything is quiet. I sit down with my back against the boulder and wait.

I don't like anyone. I don't like anyone because no one likes me. If no one likes me, then no one regards me as pleasant or enjoys my company or has a positive opinion about me. If no one is no person at all, then Rachel and Floyd don't like me. If anyone is any person at all, then I don't like Rachel and Floyd...but I want Rachel and Floyd to like me.

There is a stabbing pain in the bottom of my stomach.

If I'm sick, then I'm affected by an illness, or I have a psychiatric disorder that makes me dangerous to others, or I'm spiritually or emotionally distraught, or I'm utterly tired of something because of having had too much of it, or I'm feeling deep or passionate longing for something or somebody, or I'm filled with disgust or repulsion...

I stand up. I come out from behind the boulder and work my way back through the trees. I work my way back and work my way back. I work my way back, but I can't find the trail. I hack through the trees, but I can't find the trail, I can't find the trail, I stop. I keep going, I stop. I keep going, I stop, I keep going I stop, then there is something, it's not my own walking or breathing, it's music.

Music is coming through the trees. Someone is singing. I follow the voice through the trees, I hack through the trees, I hack through the trees, there's a clearing ahead, with tables, tables with red-checkered tablecloths. A guitar accompanies the singer. It's David Hill. He sings, "Chip, Chip, Jesus will find you / Chip, Chip, he's right behind you..." There are no people in the clearing, only tables and garbage cans. I step out of the trees into the clearing.

62

I walk across the clearing toward the music. A row of heads and backs appears. I head for an empty bench in the back on the right side. The amphitheater slopes down. Students and instructors and ranch hands are sitting on several rows of semicircular wooden benches watching David Hill. David Hill is sitting in a chair on the ground in front of a large, circular, stone fire pit. There's a black curtain or sheet hanging between tree branches to the ground off stage to the right. I sit down. A fire is burning in the pit, and there are different colored lights on in the trees. It is still daylight. Rachel is sitting in the front row on the left side. Floyd and Cosmic and Jolly are sitting in the back row on the left side.

"Chip, Chip, Chip / Braving the wilderness alone. Chip, Chip, Chip / Jesus will carry you home," David Hill sings. He sings "home" for a long time and holds his right arm out over his guitar. The note fades; his head falls onto his chest. Some people clap. "In Jesus' name we pray," he says, unplugs his guitar, stands up, and walks off stage to the left. He puts the guitar in a case and sits down in the front row next to Rachel.

The black sheet moves. It moves again. David Hill gets up, walks over and leans into the microphone. "Please welcome our guest, Blackcorn, Storyteller," he says and sits down. Some people clap.

Something flies over the black sheet, lands on the ground in front of it, and rolls in front of the fire pit. It's hissing; it has a fuse. A second thing flies over the black curtain, lands on the ground, but doesn't roll. It's hissing; it has a fuse too. The second one pops; it's a firecracker. Then the first one, the ball, starts emitting a thick stream of black smoke.

Blackcorn, Storyteller emerges from behind the black sheet. He's a black man. We are the only two black men here. He's wearing a light blue and white-checkered little girl's dress over regular clothes: a dark blue t-shirt, black pants, and work boots. He has on a light blue and white-checkered bonnet and carries a white hooked staff. He meanders around in and out of the smoke, looking at the audience each time he makes a turn. The smoke tapers off. He stops in front of the fire pit. Some of the kids are laughing.

Blackcorn aims his crook at the crowd. "Shut the fuck up!" he says. The kids stop laughing. David Hill stands up. Blackcorn points his crook at David Hill. "Sit down, pussy! This is my show!" David Hill puts his hands on his hips. "Sit down!" David Hill sits down. Blackcorn reaches under his dress and pulls papers out of one of his back pants pockets. He holds up the papers. "Contract. Signed. Says, 'Blackcorn does and says whatever the hell he wants. Because it's *art*.'" He puts the papers back in his pocket and turns around. "And get this shit outta here. I don't need this shit." He punches the microphone. It makes a loud thud in the speakers. The microphone and stand fall over and hit the ground. There's another loud thud. A hi-pitched tone comes through the speakers. He kicks the folding chair. It flies into the air and hits the ground folded. The hi-pitched tone gets louder and louder. I put my hands over my ears. People put their hands over their ears and cry out for it to stop.

Blackcorn walks behind the fire pit and stops. David Hill and his students get up and clear the chair and the microphone and the microphone stand from the stage. The piercing noise stops. Everybody's talking. Blackcorn walks in front of the fire pit. He holds his arms and his crook up then brings them slowly down. Everyone gets quiet.

"Okay," Blackcorn says and smiles. "Now we got all the housekeeping out the way, we can get down to business. I am, as you know from that very warm and generous introduction, Blackcorn, Storyteller. So. Guess what I'm fixin' to do?"

"Tell a story," someone yells.

"Yeah, that's right." Blackcorn starts walking. "I'm fixin' to tell y'all a little story." He stops. "Anybody want to guess what that story going to be about?"

"Bo Peep, Little Bo Peep," people say.

"That's right. How'd you guess?" Everyone laughs. Blackcorn puts his hand to his chin and walks. "Okay, well let's see...how to begin..." He stops and holds up a finger. "Hey, I know...once upon a time. Yeah, once upon a time," he says and walks. He reaches under his dress into his other back pocket and pulls out a flask. He stops, takes a sip, puts it back, and walks.

"Once upon a time, there was a young lady name Bo Peep. She lived on the outskirts of town, in a tiny village, in a tiny house with her momma, Sandra Peep; her daddy, Jimmy Peep; and her little brother, Mo Peep. Everybody in the village was related in some way or another, and they was all of 'em poor. Jimmy Peep worked sixteen hours a day, seven days a week at the Duncan Yo-Yo factory in town, and Sandra Peep worked all day every day cleaning city folk's houses. This meant a lot of times, especially during the summer, Bo had to look after Mo.

"Bo got good at thinking shit up for them to do too: pad-a-cake pad-a-cake, marbles, hide-and-seek, horsey-on-the-leg. Mostly, though, Mo just liked fucking around with his yo-yo – he took his red Duncan Imperial with him everywhere he went – and he liked running around outside; he especially liked playing down by the creek at the bottom of the hill from Old Mother Hubbard's house. Bo liked going outside too because while Mo was running around and whatnot, she could lie down in the grass and look up at the sky and dream. Momma warned Bo, in regards to these excursions, 'You keep an eye on your brother now. Don't let him out of your sight. And don't wander up the hill too close to Old Mother Hubbard's. I used to clean her house; that lady ain't right.' Bo wasn't worried, though. She figured she knew more about watching over Mo than her momma did at this point in time, and she wasn't about to be scared of some old lady who ain't even come out her own house in the last ten years. Besides, Old Mother Hubbard's was on the other side of the creek, it was too deep to cross on foot, and there was no bridge or log across it anywhere.

Blackcorn reaches into his back pocket and gets his flask. He stops and takes a drink. He puts it back and continues, "So. One day, Bo and Mo go down by the creek. Mo, as usual, commences to mess around the banks; and Bo, as usual, lies down in the grass and looks up at the sky. In a couple minutes, though, something *un*usual happens: Bo's eyes start to get heavy; they start to sag, and before she knows it, she asleep. When she wakes up, Mo is gone.

"Bo calls his name, but there's no answer. She runs down the creek one direction: nothing. Then she runs down the creek the other direction, and much to her consternation, there's a big two-by-four stretching across the creek. She crosses it and runs around on the other side calling Mo's name. But still, no answer. She looks up at Old Mother Hubbard's house, sitting all dark on top of that hill. She's scared now.

"But she calls up the courage – she got to – and she goes up there and rings the old lady's bell. It goes, 'Ding-dong', and she waits. Nobody comes to the door. She rings it again, 'Ding-dong'. She waits. Nobody. Bo tries one more time and gives up. She cries, 'Wah wah wah,' all the way home.

"Now, when Bo got home and told her momma and daddy the bad news, they was upset. Her momma fell to her knees and cried, 'I told you, I told you never to take your eyes off a that boy and never get too close to that Old Mother Hubbard's. Oh Lord, Oh Lord. You get him back, Bo. You find a way to get him back or be a curse to this family forever.' Momma was upset. Bo cried too and ran to her daddy for solace. He took Bo in his arms and rocked her like a little baby. 'Shh, shh, little one,' he said. 'It's going to be all right.'

"The first thing daddy did was call the whole village together at the church, and when everybody heard what had happened, they dropped whatever it was they was doing and went out into the hills and fields to look for Mo. They searched high and low until it got dark, but there was no sign of Mo anywhere. When they got back at the church, everybody was saying,' It had to been Old Mother Hubbard; it had to been Old Mother Hubbard snatched up Mo and locked him inside her house; we got to get up there and break down her door'. 'Wait a minute, wait a minute', Reverend Dixon said, trying to act the voice of reason. 'Why in the world would Old Mother Hubbard go and do something like that?' Bo's momma stood up with tears all over her puffy red face and cried, 'Because she eats children, Reverend! Don't you know?' And the whole congregation ran amok until Bo's daddy stood up and said, 'Hold up! Hold up, goddammit! I got a plan, I got a plan!'

"Everybody calmed down and Jimmy Peep explained that there was this white dude name of Hardiman just started working with him down at the yo-yo factory. He said Hardiman had just got out of jail for being a thief, but that he had not repented the error of his ways therein, and was always bragging about breaking into city folks houses and stealing stuff and about how much he enjoyed doing that. Jimmy Peep said what he was going to do was work a bunch of overtime shifts and pay Hardiman to bust into Old Mother Hubbard's house and either get Mo out of there, or collect some kind of evidence that he can give to the sheriff that Mo is, indeed, stuck up in there. Everybody agreed and Jimmy Peep got to work. In the meantime, Bo's momma suffered visions of Mo's incarceration in Old Mother Hubbard's house, and everybody in the village treated Bo as a pariah.

"Then one morning Bo woke up and came out of her room, and there was a red Duncan Imperial yo-yo lying on the breakfast table. Bo's momma was sitting there crying. 'No sign of Mo,' Bo's daddy said, 'but he did find this. I'm heading down to the sheriff's now,' Bo's daddy said. Bo cried. Jimmy Peep left and Bo and her momma hugged and cried some more and became very hopeful that the sheriff was going to help them and that pretty soon Mo would be coming home. But when Bo's daddy returned, their hopes were dashed. The sheriff had told him that the yo-yo had been illegally obtained and was thus not admissible as evidence against Mrs. Hubbard, and that even if it had been legally obtained, the yo-yo would not amount to probable cause for a search warrant because it wasn't unique; there was nothing on it to identify it as Mo's. Everybody in town's got a red Duncan Imperial just like that one, the sheriff told Bo's daddy. 'You all have patience. We'll find your Mo,' he said.

"But Jimmy and Sandra Peep didn't have no more patience, and when they told everybody else in the village what the sheriff had said, they didn't have no more patience either. In fact, they was all enraged, and it was then and there agreed: that night they would all of them, the whole village, march over to Old Mother Hubbard's, break her door down, kill her, get Mo out of there, and burn the place to the ground.

"And sure enough, once the sun had set, the villagers raised up their torches and, with Little Bo Peep in the lead, marched over to Old Mother Hubbard's. They assembled outside Old Mother Hubbard's, but before they commenced to beat down the door, Reverend Dixon raised up his voice and said, 'The path of the righteous man is beset on all sides by the inequities of the selfish and the tyranny of evil men. Blessed is he, who in the name of charity and goodwill, shepherds the weak through the valley of darkness, for he is truly his brother's keeper and the finder of lost children. And I will strike down upon thee with great vengeance and furious anger those who would attempt to poison and destroy my brothers. And you will know my name is the Lord when I lay my vengeance upon thee.'

"The men of the village then carry back the great black pole they had fashioned for the occasion, and the women and children make a path."

Blackcorn, standing behind the fire pit, reaches into the front pocket of his dress and pulls out a handful of something. It falls between his fingers. Dust. He raises it above his head, above the fire, and holds it there.

"The men charge forward with the pole, but Old Mother Hubbard has a charge of her own, and just as they hit the door..."

Blackcorn throws the dust into the fire, there's a huge explosion of smoke and flame, people scream and fall backwards out of their seats, smoke blows out all over, orange flames rise high out of the fire pit, I stand up, lots of people stand up, confused, watching, waiting until...

The flames recede.

The smoke clears.

Blackcorn is gone.

The black sheet in the trees is gone.

Everything is quiet.

People start to clap.

Everybody claps and yells.

Someone puts a piece of paper into my hand.

I look around.

The person is gone.

I unfold the paper.

It says, "Meet me under hay bail mountain now – Rachel."

63

"Meet me under hay bail mountain now – Rachel."
"Meet me under hay bail mountain now – Rachel."

Rachel, Rachel, if Rachel wants to meet me, then she wants to get together with me, she wants to have a relationship with me, she wants to have an emotionally close friendship involving sexual relations with me under hay bail mountain.

I step over the bench and cross the clearing, there is no one in front of me, I reach the trail and run, I run down the trail, under the trees, toward the ranch, I stumble, it is still daylight, but it is darker on the trail, in the trees, the sun is beginning to go down, I run, I run past Rudy Dude's, past The Big House and into the road, I pass the dining hall and hear yelling, it's coming from the Mexican bunkhouses, I keep running, there's a group of Mexicans standing in a circle around Rudy Dude, they're all talking a lot, they're talking loud, they're yelling, I slow down.

If they're yelling, then they're shouting or screaming or crying, if they're shouting, then they're speaking in an angry voice, and if they're angry, then they're feeling extremely annoyed, if they're screaming, then they're uttering a loud piercing high-pitched cries in fear, pain, desperation, or excitement, and if they're crying, then they're uttering loud, inarticulate expressions of rage, pain, or surprise.

Maria steps back from the group, she turns to me and wipes her hands on her apron, I stop. She rejoins the group, I walk toward the shed.

I walk into the shed and over to hay bail mountain, I go under hay bail mountain, I sit down on a bail of hay and wait.

David Hill comes around the corner carrying a shovel in one hand, I stand up, he stops, his face is tight and red, his eyes are swollen, he sniffs, "All right, Birdsong," he says, "Now I'm going to teach you to keep your big black dick off my sister," he takes off his black cowboy hat and puts it on a hay bail, he takes up the shovel into both hands and sniffs and comes toward me he takes the shovel back he swings the blade I fall backwards the blade grazes my shirt I fall onto hay bails David Hill takes the blade up I roll to the left the blade comes down I jump off the hay bails and run out of the mountain into the shed I run to the door and grab my rake turn and raise it he comes out of the mountain he runs toward me I run out of the shed and stand on the other side of the door I take the rake up he runs out of the shed and stops I swing the rake down the teeth sink into the back of his head they stay there I pull the rake his head pulls back with it I let go he screams and stumbles he falls onto the mountain of rocks and slides down it all of the rocks of the mountain start sliding and falling out of the circle they slide and they fall more and more it gets louder and louder thousands and thousands of sliding rocks falling and striking each other I.

64

jailbird

A fat man in a white shirt is walking away to the right across the field below. He's halfway across. He's getting smaller. He is walking toward a large building at the far end of the field. He disappears behind the large building.

It's dark, but, in the distance, to the left of the large building, there is some blue in the sky. Above, the moon is out and full. The air is silver; everything is silver. Everything is very pleasing and makes a deep and favorable impression on my mind and senses.

Two red lights come on in the dark to the right of the large building. They move; they move away. It's a car, or truck, or other road vehicle. The red lights go from side to side with a slow gentle rhythm over the invisible landscape. They come to a standstill. They go a short distance and come to a standstill again. The vehicle turns left. The two red lights turn into one, and white headlights appear. There is a mountain behind the vehicle; the mountain is darker than the sky. The vehicle moves increasingly quickly through the darkness at the bottom of the mountain. The fat man is getting away from this place with great or excessive haste.

Across the field, to the left of the large building, there are other shorter buildings and structures with yellow lights on them. Next to one of the structures, there is a group of lights. The lights are orange and burning or shining unsteadily, producing flames or on fire. There's movement; the lights are moving around the way in which a large number of people trying to achieve something moves. It's a group of people who are doing something together. It's a party.

Below and to my left, in a clearing in the trees at the foot of the mountain, there is a fire in a fire pit and two tents: one large, one small. People are living outdoors as a recreational activity, but there is no work, or movement, or anything that anyone is doing. The camp has no occupants, or all the occupants are asleep inside the tents.

I am in a wooden box. I'm sitting in a wooden chair in a wooden box that's raised up off the ground fifteen, twenty feet. My knees are touching the wall in front of me. On the wall above my knees is written, "You are in the Dude Ranch jail." I am in a secure place for keeping people awaiting legal judgment. I look at my arms. I am black. I am a black man. But who am I? I don't know. I don't know my name. I don't know who I am...

I turn my head one way then the other. The rectangular opening runs all the way around the box. I move my legs to the left of the chair and stand up. The chair hits one wall; I am standing against the opposite wall. Behind the chair, in the floor, is a door. Behind the door is a wall. I push the door with my foot. It moves, but it's locked, locked from the outside. I stand on top of the door. I touch the roof.

The box is small in size but offers a comfortable well-arranged space; it is quiet and private and secluded; it is free from stress or anxiety. In the box, I feel no strain or tension; no anxiety, pressure, or sense of threat; no awkwardness, stiffness, or self-consciousness. I feel free from problems, worry, or pain.

There are voices. I go back to the chair and sit. There is someone new at the far end of the field to the right.

The voices are coming from the left, from a notch in the mountain behind the campsite. The voices are male.

The person at the far end of the field is coming.

The men are screaming and yelling and laughing in a wild and uncontrolled way, with an extraordinary degree of intensity. They are ripped, unstable, hostile, deranged.

The person coming is wearing a white doctor's coat.

The men come around the notch. They are in and out of the trees.

The person coming is wearing a white doctor's coat and is tall and thin.

The men are heading for the campsite. There are three of them: one is in a wheelchair; one is abnormally white; the other one is short.

The person coming is wearing a white doctor's coat and a tie, and he is a tall, thin, bald man.

The abnormally white man stops and points.

The man in the white doctor's coat is wearing glasses. He is over halfway across the field.

The abnormally white man gets down on the left side of the wheelchair; the short man kneels on the right. He's putting something in the right hand of the man in the wheelchair. The short man extends his arm in front of the man in the wheelchair, away from the man in the wheelchair. He's pushing something in front of the man in the wheelchair. It's a bow. It's a bow and arrow. The bow is bent. The string is tight.

The man in the white doctor's coat approaches.

Acknowledgments

Thanks to Michael Schmidt, Elizabeth Reeder, Toby Litt, Helen Stoddart, Jane Goldman, Chris Lura, Joseph Lease, Heather Cuthbertson, Miranda Mellis, Kevin Killian, Cooley Windsor, Jeremy Horton, James Edwards, Rick Thompson, Squid, Nick Courtright, and, of course, Jennifer and Edie Guest; also, *Paul Revere's Horse*, *Gold Man Review*, The University of Glasgow (UK), California College of the Arts, Rice University, The Trap Bar (Targhee!), and Winter Park Pub.

Also, the exchange at the end of chapter 54 is adapted in parody from Stanley Kubrick's 1968 film, *2001: A Space Odyssey*.

About the Author

Graham Guest has lived in Northern California with his wife and daughter since 2012. He teaches in the Literature and Languages Department at Dominican University of California. His band, Moses Guest, is still making music. Learn more at graham-guest.com.